About the Author

THE AUTHOR is born and educated in Newton Abbot, Devon. Now single and pursuing a new venture of creative arts. This quiet hobby takes her to an imaginative and exciting place to write these stories.

The Delightful Mrs Clara Fortesque

Marianna Shore

The Delightful Mrs Clara Fortesque

Olympia Publishers
London

www.olympiapublishers.com
OLYMPIA PAPERBACK EDITION

Copyright © Marianna Shore 2024

The right of Marianna Shore to be identified as author of
this work has been asserted in accordance with sections 77 and 78 of
the Copyright, Designs and Patents Act 1988.

All Rights Reserved

No reproduction, copy or transmission of this publication
may be made without written permission.
No paragraph of this publication may be reproduced,
copied or transmitted save with the written permission of the publisher,
or in accordance with the provisions
of the Copyright Act 1956 (as amended).

Any person who commits any unauthorised act in relation to
this publication may be liable to criminal
prosecution and civil claims for damage.

A CIP catalogue record for this title is
available from the British Library.

ISBN: 978-1-80439-862-3

This is a work of fiction.
Names, characters, places and incidents originate from the writer's
imagination. Any resemblance to actual persons, living or dead, is
purely coincidental.

First Published in 2024

Olympia Publishers
Tallis House
2 Tallis Street
London
EC4Y 0AB

Printed in Great Britain

Dedication

The reader of this book: I hope this novel brings you to a time and place, with this lovely lady, who is happy and a pleasure to be with.

Acknowledgements

Thank you, Olympia Publishers, and all the teams working on my novel. Without their help and encouragement, I would not have fulfilled my dream in having this novel published.

CHAPTER 1

After lunch, Clara heads outside, to do some gardening, later on today, she will be going out to the Hill Top Café, there at the café, Clara is often served by a young waitress called Emily, she has served Clara for several years. Emily has grown very fond of Clara, she looks upon her as her Granny, although Emily did have her own Gran, on her mother's side, she still enjoys Clara, she is different from Emily's Gran, she cannot pinpoint why, Emily also enjoys another older people company as well, she needs to be patient, as many elderly ladies and gentlemen, come to this quaint café, it is a quiet café, which the older generations prefer, passing the time away, chatting and catching up with their friends.

Emily knew that older people, cannot be rushed, she realises they need patient and understanding, but this café caters for all ages; some younger people arrive from time to time.

Emily is employed by two old ladies, who own it together, Bunty and Maureen, Bunty's nephew Tom, a big lad, in his thirties, unmarried, a lovely young man, by all accounts, Tom likes to give his aunty Bunty physical help, occasionally lifting the heavy sacks of flour, that are needed in cooking, especially breads, rolls and some cakes. Bunty spoils Tom, and his family, with bread that has not been sold, that day. Tom's favourite cake is the Lardy Cake, which he shares, with his girlfriend, Beth, on Saturday she serves the customers, in this café, to earn some extra pocket money, when Emily has her days off.

Bunty is also known as Auntie Bun! Which is a joke to Emily, especially as she owns the café, baking cakes and buns! Maureen is called Auntie Mo, these names are friendly to the customers, who feel the café has a homely, atmosphere about it. Maureen and Bunty, the owners are never seen, always baking, in their warm homely kitchen, organising the cakes, buns, biscuits, and wholesome brown bread making, doing their delicious cucumber sandwiches, and smoked ham and egg, which are many of their special sandwiches, amongst the coffee and walnut cakes, are a great favourite, while, the carrot cake, appeals to the younger ones, the chocolate cake and fudge cake, are the children's favourite, when arriving with their grandparents, the fruit cake is most popular in December, they serve the Christmas cake, on the twenty fifth and twenty-six of December.

Bunty and Maureen are happy, chatting, cooking, and serving numerous pots of tea, coffee, and other beverages, served on tables, with their fresh white cotton, and red check table cloths, the tea is served in silver tea pots, alongside bowls of white sugar lumps, the brown sugar lumps, preferably best, accomplished with freshly ground roasted coffee, applied with silver tongs, alongside this are served with a buttery shortbread biscuits tucked on side of the saucer. Now waiting to go out Clara is in the garden, kneeling down on her velvet green cushion, to tend to the weeds, that have sprung up, after a shower of rain overnight, Clara loved some of her garden, but not all of it, her favourite part, is the perfumed area, with the beautiful perfumed white jasmine, night scented stocks, colourful sweet peas, and lavender bushes.

She loved making useful items of objects, which make her enjoyable doing them, and happy giving other people pleasure, with using them. Clara makes her lavender pouches, from the old flower heads of the lavender, dried them, and put into little pouches, (lightweight materials, cut into small squares) sometimes selling in Markets on her own stall, or Country fairs, that come to her village, every year.

She also has a gooseberry bush, which she did not like, as the spikes are sharp and pointy, giving her sharp digs, into her skin, when pruning the bushes, the gooseberries are very sour, to eat, but Clara add lots of sugar, to enjoy them, when making a gooseberry pie and crumbles. Clara is well known for making her chutneys, jams and pickles, her source of her produce is always home grown, from the back of the garden, her vegetables, onions, tomatoes. The potatoes, she digs up, occasionally having a robin, perched on her spade, watching her, while she gropes deep, into the soil for new potatoes, the tomatoes are sometimes grown indoors in her warm porchway. Clara has several apples trees, Bramley which are suitable for cooking, always sour, but excellent for pies and crumbles, but need sugar added, the eater apples, that Clara has no name, for they were in Clara's garden, before she moved there, every year, she would go along to a big field, in August, which is not far from her house, and take *a large brown paper bag given to her by the grocer, when she buys other vegetables, she needs from time to time*, she can then pick pounds of blackberries, for bramble jam, blackberry and apple pies and crumbles, sometimes giving her pies and crumbles, for friends and neighbours, or taking them to the fairs alongside her chutneys, jams and pickles.

Another of Clara's problems in the garden, is her hedge, running alongside her house, over the years, this has grown more and more difficult to cut, it has grown so high, that a ladder is always needed, this is not Clara favourite activity, more new hedge-grow plants would appear, making the hedge grow thick and strong. Branches are difficult to cut, as they are always so high up, on the hedge.

'I must find a gardener to cut my hedge, and once it is lower, then the next year I can maybe manage it myself. Clara looks down at her watch, and checks the time, as well as her recently new sun dial, it is pointing to the time, she has educated herself by watching the sun, and her watch, where the mark on the top of it is, pointing to half past two, I love this sundial, only lets me down when it is raining, when I am indoors with my watch, and the mantlepiece clock, perhaps I will treat myself to a cuckoo clock one day, this will wake me up, if I drop off to sleep, in the afternoon in the lounge, phew! all this work has made me forget the time.

CHAPTER 2

Clara, was just thinking about going, indoors to get ready to go out, when she heard someone calling out her name. *I am not expecting anyone,* thought Clara to herself.

'Yoo-hoo! hello, are you there, Mrs Fortesque, I can hear someone digging just now, is that you in your garden,' shouts a man's voice, from the other side of the hedge.

'Hello! Yes, I was digging just now,' replied Clara shouting back, who on earth is that, Clara was very puzzled, not seeing who it was, she could not think who this could be.

She thought she would investigate, and find out, she strolled out towards the garden gate, and looks up and down the road, behind the hedge, she saw was an elderly man, bending down stroking a tortoiseshell fully grown cat.

'Why, hello, was that, you are calling out to me' inquired Clara, *it's my neighbour from number 46.*

'Yes! it is me' replies the man. walking towards Clara's gate.

'How are you? Mrs Fortesque?' he asked sprightly.

'I am fine, how are you?' Clara answering back, watching him marching briskly towards her.

Eventually he arrived at Clara's gate.

He was slightly puffed out, 'I am fine, but my wife is unwell, could I ask you for a favour,' he said.

'Yes, I am good at doing favours to people, what is it you want,' enquired Clara, rather puzzled to what Mr Dawson wanted to ask her to do.

'Could you to stay with my wife one afternoon, while, I go to and see my daughter,

My wife's stepdaughter Susan, she lives a long way from here, I require to be away a whole afternoon,' asks Mr Dawson anxiously.

'Of course, I would love to, just say the day, I am sure I can fit her in, now what is your wife called, let me think, is it Delia?' asked Clara, remembering.

'Yes, it is Delia, but she likes to be called Del as soon as that possible,' asked Mr Dawson.

'Yes of course, anything for a neighbour, I hope your wife is going to get better, but I have to check my diary, in case I need to be somewhere else,' declared Clara.

'Yes, thank you, she has strained her ankle, with a few bruises, very painful, her foot is propped up on a stool, she does not want to stand on it, in fact I insist she stays put, she was up, on the ladder, reaching for a book, on the top shelf in our study, she heard the phone ringing, and rushed down the ladder quickly, then rather awkwardly twisting her ankle. We usually both go together, to see Susan regularly, every Saturday, her husband is away at sea, he is in the Navy, and poor.'

Susan get very lonely, I cannot let her down, Del cannot possibly come over with me.

Susan is very upset that Delia, that she cannot see her this week, Susan was upset to hear about Delia's ankle.

Del, does like your company, Mrs Fortesque, you have so much to tell her, your family. The Fortesque, you go to, your involvement with the WI, Delia's friend Harriette, who used to stay weeks with us sometimes, she liked Harriette, but now, she has got married, she can only stay an hour with Del, due to her husband coming home, and expects his wife to be there, when he comes in, and you do make her laugh, laughter is the best medicine isn't it, Mrs Fortesque, admits Mr Dawson.

'Yes, I agree,' says Mrs Fortesque, flicking a fly off, that landed on her face.

I am sorry to ask you, but my wife is adamant to see you. Your humour is a tonic; especially the story, she tells me about the time you rode on a horse in the New Forest, and you came across a deer, with her foal, and you unmounted your horse, and came over to stroke them. They both ran away, your horse bolted and left you alone without a horse and you had to walk miles to go to the stables, and explain you lost your horse they found the horse, miles away munching grass on a nearside road.

You never went riding in the New Forest again, and the horse that bolted was called Lightning, that was funny too? Wasn't it,

Also, your talks with the WI, and your tales with the time you used to work at a florist, and had them make up a bouquet for a dog lover Mrs Fortesque grinned Mr Dawson.

'Yes, it was difficult making a dog shape bouquet,' admitted Clara, giggling.

Yes, I did your husbands will, do you remember Mrs Fortesque, I worked in Leyton, the town you came to our premises, Thomas and sons, Solicitor is next to a bakery,

'Yes, I remember, Michael and I bought our bread, from that shop is it called 'Use Your loaf,' it sells all kinds of breads, even baby sizes, in small Hovis tins, my children used to play Mummy and Daddies, and this bread with my home-made jam which was their tea time food with the dolls being the children, of course the dolls did not eat the bread and jam, just my children. Oh it brings back happy times with their baby size tea service, and the pretend food was made of Plaster of Paris from the toy shop in the market. Every week we bought our lardy cake from them delicious as it oozed sweet syrup.

I must stop talking, this is not going anywhere, I will dash inside and check my diary.

Mr Dawson, to make sure I have no commitments on that day Clara looked down at her watch noticed the time *it* is nearly time for my four o'clock tea now where is my diary.

Clara, rushes in to the lounge, and finds her diary from the drawer, it was in the drawer, that next to one that holds Clara's silver service, and tablecloths, underneath the tablecloths, safe and out *of harm's way.*

'Aha! here it is, Clara sits down for a minute, she to flips through her diary, I am doing something but not sure what I am doing. What shall I say, I must have my tea on that day, Clara rushed out to Mr Dawson.

'I will be awfully grateful, if you can come over, Delia is so looking forward to seeing you, he asked anxiously.'

'If it is a Thursday, I am busy and have plans,' admitted Clara, and looks at the clock.

'Oh! no, I can do any other day what about Sunday,' asked Clara hurrily.

'It cannot be Sunday, we go to church,' said Mr Dawson sadly.

I can do this Wednesday next week, my diary said I was going to a Market fair, but I was informed that it may be cancelled. So that will be okay with me, I can do,' informed Clara.

'Good, I will ring Susan, as say I can make the Wednesday the eleventh,' said Mr Dawson pleased that Clara could make one day.

'Excellent she will tell you about her embroidery classes, at the moment, she is knitting a jersey for me, she says it is surprise one, but I know she is going to knit me a jersey with a kitten on the front, just like the one, we lost last year, Smoky, our grey kitten with white socks on his feet, not real ones, but his paws have marks like white socks on,' said Mr Dawson.

'I will look forward to seeing Delia, no sorry Del stories, but our WI moved to another town, Michael used to take me there, as I do not drive, I could go on the bus, but coming back on my own, is no fun, sometimes in the winter, the nights drawing in, and I get nervous on the buses alone, walking home, is not pleasant, with some stranger following me, very scary, then that had to go, his faithful old Austin Betty, that is what he called his car (it was an old car).

'Can you make after one fifteen, it will give me time, to inform you about the house, or any details about her condition, whether Del, can do anything other, then put her ankle up on the stool, I will look forward to you coming Mrs Fortesque,' admitted Mr Dawson, smiling.

'I will be over then,' said Clara, pleased to be useful for a neighbour.

Mr Dawson left Clara, and went happily homewards back to Del.

Clara watched Mr Dawson, strolling happily down the road.

'That makes me very happy,' admitted Clara, smiling.

Clara went inside, and felt contented to do her mission, on the Wednesday, the following week.

CHAPTER 3

This morning Clara knew, this was the day, as a good neighbour, she was going to help Delia who needed her, luckily it turned out to be a bright and cheerful day, a good time to be going out, which will help Delia, cheer her up, if she is able to see the sun shining.

Now downstairs, in her pink candlewick dressing gown, and her blue fluffy slippers, Clara wanders into the kitchen, to have her breakfast, cornflake cereal, followed by one slice of brown toast, covered with a smear of butter, and a teaspoon of marmalade, the thick sort, her breakfast tea blend, with a dash of milk, followed by a small glass of freshly squeezed orange juice, now she is almost ready for helping her neighbour Delia, assisting her, and staying with her, while her husband is out all day.

In the lounge, she thought about her duties, with Delia, she has never done this before, and has no idea what lies ahead, it cannot be difficult talking to a neighbour, and helping her, if she needed any assistant, just be cheerful, and do not say No, at any point, Delia is relying on you, to be a strong and a capable person, just put your best foot forward, and be there, and if Delia needs anything that requires doing.

Clara, switched on the radio, enjoying the morning concert, then changing over later, to another radio station, to hear a play, about Freddie going on a train, to see his Mother, on her birthday, the radio programme, finished right on time, for her to be going out, she made herself a ham and hot mustard sandwich, then thought that it was the right time, that Mr Dawson wanted her over there, getting in good time, before he boarded the train, the clock on the mantlepiece, was just after one o'clock.

Mr Dawson required me, just before he catches the train, he asked me, if I could make it one fifteen, to come over, which I said I could.

Clara went upstairs, to the bathroom, cleaning her teeth, and washing her face first, then into the bedroom, changed into her day clothes, she turned down the sheets, to air the bed, then making sure upstairs was sorted, she came downstairs checking, the down side of the house, washing, up her breakfast things, and last night dinner plate, a dessert bowl, knife, fork and spoon, a glass of water, her cup, she used for her cocoa drink. She secured the back door, bolted it from the inside, checked the windows, making sure they were all shut tight, when she was happy, with all the security checks, she put on her coat.

Her front door, has a thick heavy key, this is her old Victorian house, she is now living in now, Clara decided to change her old lock for a Yale lock, to be more secure kind, she had to purchase a different lock with a new key, it was an old the old fashion lock before, which was nice to look at, but if she lost this key, would be difficult to purchase a new one, after she had her new lock fitted, she thought she would treat herself, with a silver keyring fob, with her own initials on it. Her initials are C. V. L. F.

She wanted to keep hold of her heavy old metal key, so she could look at it from time to time, as this key, was an antique one, which she could display, in her much-loved cabinet now, if she moved to a new house, this would have a been a keepsake, on her lovely old house. 'The Grange' with several other pieces, of precious items, which were nostalgic to Clara, but to anyone else, just an old key. this memorability's was the only one, who would treasure it.

'Right! house, we will leave you for a few hours, then I will be back to get my dinner, and dessert, when I eventually get back home,'

'Clara looked in her hallway mirror, to check whether her face looked okay, making sure she was clean and respectable examining her hair, that was okay, now off we go,' she said smiling to herself.

She slammed the front door, behind her, stepping down from her one step, and proceeds down the road, towards number forty-six Marigold Road, Clara had to walk past eight houses, before reaching Mr Mrs Dawson home, she then past several lovely houses on the way, but secretly Clara knew, she has the prettiest house in the road.

Arriving at the gate of number 46, she opens it she proceeded down the path, as she marched down towards the house, high up in the tree, a chirping sound was heard, a song thrush who was merrily singing on his own, perched high up on a branch of an old apple tree, nearby. Clara reached the red door of number 46, she looks around for a bell, but there was only a brass knocker, she wrapped sharply on the door, and waited, looking back at their garden, watching the song thrush in the tree, Clara heard footsteps coming, towards the door, when eventually the door opened, Mr Dawson stood there smiling, at the much-needed presence of Clara, so he could see his daughter Susan, he was looking very handsome, tidy and dapper, in his brown suit, and white shirt, blue tie and brown matching trousers. Clara thought he was very fetching for his age.

Mr Dawson uttered to Clara, saying, 'spot on time Mrs Fortesque, Del is waiting for you in the lounge, please come on in.'

'Thanks, I am looking forward to this day, not many people ask me to do, them a favour, these days,' admitted Clara, smiling.

As she stepped in she noticed on the walls some beautiful pictures of landscape, a seascape, and a picture of a lady, whom Clara recognised, she was also admiring the décor of their house.

Mr Dawson noticed Clara standing, looking around at his painting on the walls, he then mentioned, and pointing out to a large picture on the wall opposite.

'That picture over there, is of my dear wife Del, painted by a local artist,' he Proudly mentioned, with a slight tear in his eyes, he carefully wiped his eyes with his finger, very discreetly.

'What a beautiful woman your wife is, I have only seen her a couple of times, while she was pottering around in your garden, when I walked to the shops sometimes,' admitted Clara noticing Mr Dawson sad face, looking half happy, half sad.

'Thank you, I think she is beautiful too, but I married her, not for her looks, but for her sweet nature,' admitted Mr Dawson, now looking happier than he was a minute ago, talking about his beautiful and kind wife.

' Lovely she is,' admitted Clara agreeing with him, still looking at this picture.

'Follow me,' he said, beckoning Clara to follow him, as he was walking toward the lounge.

Clara spoke up, 'can I hang my coat up first,' asks Clara

stopping, as she wanted to take off her coat, hat, as Mr Dawson's house was somewhat warm, and Clara was hot after her walk to get there, Mr Dawson had the heating on as Del was sat still, and sometimes felt the cold not moving about having to sit all day with her feet up.

'Oh, sorry, I forgot my manners,' apologised Mr Dawson.

Clara promptly took off her heavy, dark green coat, and hung it on the brass hooks nearby.

Mr Dawson waits patiently, watching Clara hang her coat up.

When Clara had hung her coat up, Mr Dawson urged Clara to follow him, he Strolled towards the lounge, with Clara following behind him.

He opened the door, in the corner sat on a mustard coloured armchair, with her one leg up, on a wooden tapestry foot stool, sat Delia, looking pleased to see Clara come in, Clara beamed across to Delia she had been cooped up indoors since last week, nursing her ankle, looking slightly tired, and white, compared to Clara who was looking strong and capable.

'Now you are here, and met Delia, can I show you Mrs Fortesque, where the tea, milk and sugar are kept, so, you can make a brew this afternoon.

'Delia piped up, Barry could you please pass me, my handkerchief,' asked Delia, feeling a sniffle coming on.

Mr Dawson, fetched Delia a handkerchief, from a pile of newly ironed sheets, and pillowcases nearby, waiting to be taken upstairs to the airing cupboard.

Clara follows Barry into the kitchen, Clara heard Delia say his name, when she asked him, to pass her a handkerchief.

Clara followed Mr Dawson into the kitchen, where he pointed out, where everything was kept, he knew that Clara was a lady of taste, who liked the best china, and he wanted to impress Clara, he made sure not give her any crack or chipped china.

Clara noticed the beautiful china, that Barry had displayed on the kitchen table, ready for their afternoon tea.

Clara commented, 'What beautiful china cups, you have Mr Dawson.'

'Only the best for Mrs Fortesque,' he admitted.

'Thank you, Barry,' expressed Clara, grinning.

He turned around back to face Clara, his face had lit up, he was not used to anyone calling him Barry only his dear wife.

They both returned to the lounge, Barry mentioned that he must dash, to catch the two fifteen train.

'Bye Delia darling' he bent over and gave his wife a quick kiss on the cheek.

'Thank you, Mrs Fortesque, for coming here today,' conveyed Mr Dawson, gratefully.

'Call, me Clara, please,' insisted Clara.

'Thank you, Clara, please stay there with her wife, you needed come out with me, I will see you later, inform my wife to behave herself, and not demand to many demands from you, all you need is to be doing is sitting with her,' he said gratefully.

'Delia, did not notice what her husband has,' said Delia, was blowing her nose, and was unaware of the conversation between Barry and Clara just then.

He left the room.

When Clara heard the door slam, she relaxed, and sat down beside Delia, on a chair, that her husband usually sits on, to be near his beloved wife.

'Now, Delia how are you today? inquired Clara, leaning

over to hear her reply,' she thought she better call her by her full name for now.

'Much better thank you Mrs Fortesque, still a bit sore, but this to be expected seeing it had my whole weight, on it when I twisted it,' replied Delia, rubbing her leg.

'Call me Clara, please, and can I call you Del ,if that is okay Delia. Now what would you like me to do for you,' she asked Delia.

'Nothing, thanks just talk about your adventures, and your family,' conveyed Delia.

'Okay, we can have a cup of tea, later, when or if I bore you, with all my chatter,' said Clara, smiling at Delia, looking at her ankle, which was still blue with her bruises.

'I am sure I won't,' admitted Delia.

'Have you bathed your ankle in a cold water yet, to help the swelling,' asked Clara.

'Yes, I did thank you, it did help a little bit, I am looking forward to you coming today, my conversation with Barry was getting a bit, empty, I can now tell him about your experiences if I may, if that is okay Clara,' asked Delia.

'I understand perfectly, I know when you are retired, you both need outside interests, to keep your marriage alive, admitted Clara, now Delia, I shall start at the very beginning, *I was married to Michael, as you know, I am now a widow, living alone in my old Victorian House, here in Huntley. I am a lady of leisure, a friendly neighbour, and a good listener, now retired, but in my younger days, lived-in South-East London, with my parents, Edith and George, George had money left to him by a rich Uncle, so he did not work, Edith used to be office worker, in a large woollen factory, but met George, my Dad in a café, while Edith, my mother, was working in an office as a* receptionist, in the City, for a big oil company.

I have kept up with the latest fashion, and trends, going to Carnaby street, having coffee with my girl-friends, I was lucky enough to be a teenager in the swinging sixties, partying, and generally being a happy teenager, and a swinging adult. I first met Michael, when he was coming to my office to meet a friend from my oil company job.

Michael loved his work with animals, but had a yearning to come to London, and be with people, which was a change from his work, and to have an intelligent conversation, with his friends in the City, animals are okay, he admitted but they are good companions, cats and dogs, but most of his animals he came across were horses, cows, and occasional a deer, from the roadside.

'He first met me, in a lift going up, I was waiting at the second floor, waiting to go down, when Michael steps out of the lift, and he noticed that I had dropped a glove on the floor beside me, he picked it up, gave it to me, and said to me, is this your glove, he also notices my blue eyes, and announced what amazing blue eyes you have,' said Michael, he was tall with thick wavy brown hair, brown eyes which also had a twinkle in his eyes, I and when he met me, one of his eyebrows went up, which

I noticed when I met him the first time, he looked straight into my eyes, Yes, it is my glove, thanks you, I did not realise that my eyes were that blue, I smiled, and thanked him for the compliment, and I went down on the lift, on my own, and Michael went to meet his friend from work.

On another day, he was waiting to go down in the lift, the same time as I was going Down.

'Oh, hello blues eyes, how are you today, we must stop

meeting like this, he said smiling again at me, I see you are going down, can I ask you are you going to that coffee bar, on the ground floor, I meet John from one of your departments,' he admitted.

'No, I am going home,' I said, wishing to go home, before having a coffee with this man, who keeps calling me blue eyes,' I did not want to go then, perhaps another time, he insisted to ask me. 'Would you like to have coffee with me before you go home,' he asked.

'Well, if you insist, my name is Clara, I told him, by now I wanted to know who this man was, who thought I had blues, thank you, I said I would be glad of something to drink, talking to people all days, makes my mouth dry, and I am glad to talk to someone other than my work colleagues, who only talk about oil shares, which I am really fed up with talking about, all the time,' I admitted.

'I will promise, I will not talk about oil shares, we can change the subject completely, just to ask how you come to have such amazing blue eyes,' he asked.

'I think I blushed, he told me he was called Michael, I am from South of the Bank' he said. 'He asked me where do want to sit,' he asked.

'What about a seat by the window,' I asked, we found a good window seat, overlooking Hyde Park, and started chatting as if I y knew, each other for ages, I had a lot to talk about, His love of travel, and walking in the Lake District, and mine too.

I would grab all my spare time with Michael, we even went travelling and to save money hitchhiked around Europe, seeing places like France, Italy, Austria, mixing with interesting people, and staying with families who took them in, we would sleep on floors of old barns, when rooms where not *unavailable.*

Michael proposed to me, when sitting in a lorry that we were in alone before the lorry driver returned, he had got out of his lorry to fill up his tank of diesel before heading for the ferry, I was busy looking out of the window of the lorry, but eventually I turned around, and Michael, asked me to marry him, he had found a ring buried in the sand, on a beach in the south of France, it was when he was lying on the towel, he noticed an uncomfortable feeling, underneath his towel, and there was a ring, he did not tell me, but hid it from me, until he had an opportunity to propose to me, and he could not wait, so he asked me while sitting in a lorry, bound for the ferry, in the Port of Calais, he gave me the engagement ring, when I finally married Michael, he came and found a job as a Vet, setting up a practise in the small village of Harley, our children went to a local primary school, after that a public school in the South.

Twenty years later Michael sadly passed away, I kept the house which we bought, when we were first married, I had some money from an Aunt, who left me enough to keep the house going, so when my grownup children upped and gone, and then come back to see me, the five-bedroom house was ready for them, with a large garden with a swing, and a tree house, for them to disappear into.

My house is a Victorian House, in the North East of the Country, with a large beautiful garden, we were married for many years, until five years ago, losing him to an unknown illness, we have two children, both have left home to travel the world, and then met their spouses while travelling in different countries, they are now living abroad.

Benny an Architect lives in Chicago, with Caroline, they do not have any children, Caroline is a doctor. Samantha lives in

South America, Belize with her husband

Chuck who is a Dentist, and their three children, Rex, fifteen years old, Katherine, who is ten years old, and Davina six years old.

Benny phones home every Sunday, to me, and Samantha ringing me, also at six o'clock in the evening, a good time for me, but of course a different time zone, in South America and Chicago now.

Delia started to yawn, Clara realised she had either bored, poor Delia or she was genuinely tired, because of lack of sleep, from the pain in her ankle.

'Del, can I make you a cup of tea,' Clara asking quietly, in case she was being sleepy, and a loud person would not be appropriate with Del, state of health.

'Oh yes please, I would really appreciate it, the room is quite warm, Barry had put the heating on, I just need one, having had lunch a few hours ago,' said Del very happy with this.

'Do you take milk and sugar?' asked Clara.

'No sugar, but milk, not to milky, or dark tea, which makes it very bitter, not to my Liking,' admitted Del.

'Right, me too, just normal tea, with no sugar,' said Clara, very happy, not to make any complicated cup of tea.'

Clara got up, and went in to the kitchen, to prepare the making of tea for Delia and herself, she was gone a good ten minutes, Clara thought they could both do with a biscuit, Clara eventually found some custard cream biscuits, tucked inside a tin marked sugar, this is different, I wonder why they are in this tin, and not a biscuit tin, I will ask her later, when she came back, she was carrying a trayful of cups of tea.

'Oh, how lovely, a cup of tea, and biscuits,' commented

Delia. smiling and sitting up, ready to enjoy a cup of tea with this lovely lady, who was willing to help her.

'I was just saying earlier, to your husband, about this painting of you in the hallway, is such a beautiful picture of you,' said Clara handing over a cup of tea to Delia.

'Oh, thank you, Clara very kind of you to say so, my husband insisted on this, he wanted a kept sake of me , in case I you know what, I do not like to say it, that word,' admitted Delia.

Yes, I know, me too, not that word, it makes me sad, when leaving my love ones behind. Just let's say he wanted to see you, when you were out shopping, and he saw this picture, in the hallway, without getting out a small photograph from his wallet.

'Yes, lets that is much nicer description,' said Delia.

'Now is there anything else, you would like me to do, now I am here,' asks Clara being useful, and happy to help this dear lady.

'Yes, is it possible, could you open the window, I would like some fresh air, Barry, forgets sometimes, I think he is worried that if he goes out, he does not want me to get cold, while he out,' admits Delia.

Clara goes across to the window, sliding the window open.

'Thank you, Clara, I can hear the birds outside, singing, now,' said Delia.

Clara sits down again.

'I think it is time, I took the cups into the kitchen' commented Clara, picking up the Tray, she arranged the cups and saucers back on the tray, and taking the tray back. Into the kitchen.

Delia shouts after Clara, 'leave the washing up for Barry,

he is fussy about the cups, and stains, he likes to wash them with a salty solution, to make sure they have been cleaned thoroughly,' Clara.,

Clara came back from the kitchen, after dropping the tray on the table.

She sits back down again.

Clara looks down at her watch, and then glances across to the clock, on the mantel piece to compare the time.

She commented, 'is that the time, it says it is five past six, your husband should be back soon.'

The room went quiet for a minute, Clara piped up, 'is that your front door opening.'

Delia, looking happy, it sounds that your Barry is back home.

Delia looked relieved that he has arrived back safe and sound.

'Yes, I think it Mr Dawson coming in, unless it is someone else', said Clara.

He breezed in, 'I see you are keeping my wife amused, she is usually asleep these days, since her ankle was sprained,' he announced.

'Yes, we had a lovely time, I probably bored your wife, with all my chatter, but we had a lovely cup of tea, and I found some custard cream biscuits in a sugar tin,' admitted Clara.

'Jolly good, but I did buy you and Delia, some chocolate digestive as a special treat, but because I was rushing failed to tell you, I am glad you found some old biscuits in our other biscuit tin, when the biscuit tin is full, we used an old sugar tin,' admitted Barry sitting down and loosening his tight tie, and eventually sat down on the seat, armrest, phew, nice to relax, and sit down, although I have sat down with Susan, the journey home, was tiring, standing for a train, was not pleasant, packed with people, and some dogs barking, children being noisy, and demanding drinks.

Mr Dawson pulled up a chair from the table nearby, then sat down next to Delia and Clara.

'Clara, left you the cups, darling, for you to washup, I told her, you like to wash them, with a salty solution,' said Delia, her ankle, started to worry her, and started to ache, bending down to touch her ankle.

'Yes, very fussy about cups,' he admitted.

'How was Susan?' asks Clara, changing the subject, and noticing that Delia, looked uncomfortable, and maybe be someone may, give her something to help the pain.

'Very well, she has just started to do evening classes in sewing,' said Barry.

' Oh, that is good, she may make some friends, and have coffee with them sometimes,' admitted Clara.

'Yes! I asked her to make Delia a dress,' grinned Barry.

Clara noticed that Delia looked as if she was in pain, 'Delia, are you okay?'

'Yes, thank you, Clara, Barry can give me an aspirin, in the minute, I feel in need of a drink of water anyway,' said Delia.

'Well I must be going, my stomach has started to rumble, I am sure you would not, like to hear that,' commented Clara getting up.

'Okay, but Clara I have bought you a little present for your kindness,' said Barry...

'I did not expect anything, it was a delight for me, to enjoy your wife's company, I done nothing much, enjoyed her company, and nice cup of tea, with your lovely custard cream biscuits.' admitted Clara.

'Here you are Clara,' said Mr Dawson, handing over to Clara a wrapped present.

'OH, I like surprises,' she admitted, taking the present from Barry, and looking at it with joy.

Clara unwrapped the present in front of both, she carefully opened the pale mauve box, with a pink bow, decorated on top, with violet flowers, painted on the top.

'Oh, It is a lovely box of violet creams, my favourites,' admitted Clara, smiling, and such a pretty box, with violets all over the cover. 'I will treasure the box, it will go on my mantlepiece at home, and I will eat the violet creams, one on each day, so I will enjoy them longer,' admitted Clara, grinning and holding the box, carefully.

Clara stands up and speaks to Delia.

'It has been a delight in our meeting, I hope you will be up and running again, when I will see you gardening, with your trowel digging 'admitted Clara.

'Come again soon, when I am better, then we can have another chat, and next time, I will cook you a cake, but I am not sure which one, what cakes do you like?' asked Delia.

'I love all cakes, along as they sweet,' grinned Clara.

'I will decide, when you come next,' admitted Delia, smiling.

Clara wandered towards the door.

'Bye Delia,' said Clara, waving as she left.

Barry follows out with Clara together.

They reach the door, Barry opens the door for them both to go through.

'I will treasure this kind gesture, of those delightful boxes of chocolates,' admitted Clara, to Barry.

Clara, she steps outside, Clara turns around to Barry,

thanks again, for the chocolate violets.

When they had left the room, Delia closed her eyes, and falls asleep.

'Bye Clara, thanks again,' he says, watching Clara saunters down the path, glad that everything went okay, and no emergencies happened, she eventually arrives back to her house The Grange' pleased to try her new key again, which she does, she shuts the door.

Putting the key back on a hook, near the door, the next time she needs it.

CHAPTER 4

After breakfast whilst in the kitchen, Clara retreats to the lounge, but the noise outside draws Clara towards the window. The noise is coming from a group of people outside, Clara sees that the group outside, look like the family from opposite, they seem to be going somewhere, hence all that commotion, I heard looks like they are going for a jaunt in their car,

'It is jammed packed with children, and their belongs,' commented Clara to herself.

I presume that the lady with them is their mum, and the other man, possibly their dad, the two children in the back of the car, looking very excited, laughing and giggling to each other, they do look very excited, I wonder where they are off, on this sunny day,' remarked Clara to herself. I should go somewhere myself not to waste this lovely sunny day, maybe a walk to the Park, seeing it is only a stone throw away, or I could catch a bus, to the country side, but I won't take that risk, as I may not get back, if the buses, are not coming back, that day, or some other problem, my best and safest option is the near one, my park.

'Clara, was still wearing her pink nightdress, and blue dressing gown, with her worn out slippers, which had slightly fallen on one side, due to her slipping them, on quickly each morning. I must invest in some new slippers, I will try that new shoe shop, that has just opened in the town, I noticed that they sell walking shoes, these are also are worn down, too much money to fork out,' Clara grumbled,

Clara proceeded upstairs, to change into her going out clothes, *which she keeps fresh and clean, for going out on special days out,* she came back down the stairs, having decided to put on a blouse, with a frilly collar, a loose skirt, her good walking shoes, (she needs new ones) then decided on looking, at her hat situation, thought her beret, navy blue, not the red one she wore to town, with her red coat, and coloured scarf.

She plonked it on the side of her head, that she unhooked off the clothes hook,

With unhooking her coat, putting it on, buttoned up the large buttons, which were easier, than the smaller ones, which was always very fiddly, when rushing to catch a bus, (very annoying) no gloves today, not needed to, warm hands already.

'Off we jolly well go,' she said to herself.

I better check my face in case, I might have some smears on my face.

'Clara stared at herself closely in the mirror, smoothing her cheeks, with her fingers, noticing how soft they were, with hardly any deep-set wrinkles, that some women of my age get,' she remarks. I am not bad for a woman of my age, looking closely again, at the mirror, and only one or two grey hairs, an unblemished skin, it does have its advantages being old, no more teenage spots, or acne as you do, in your teens.

The mirror which is situated in the hall way, that used to belong to Clara's parents, who have now departed from this world, as Clara is the only child, the mirror, was left to her, also a stone statue beautiful young girl, were all brought back to her house, from her parent's house, in the Country.

The mirror is mounted on carved wood, which also had hung brass hooks, for hats and coats.

Clara still staring at her mirror, straightened her blue beret, adjusting her coat, buttoned up her top coat button, of her mauve coat, looked down at her shoes, just to make sure she had her shoes on, and not her slippers on, which happened once, when she got flustered, when the postman came to the door last month, and as she was rushing to catch a train, the postman wondered if she could sign for a parcel, which was not for her, but for the people next door, who were out at the time, or the postman got no answer, then seeing Clara light on, the postman came knocking at her door, so signing this parcel made her late, she quickly changed from her nightclothes, into her day clothes, and forgot to change from her slippers into her shoes. Clara then proceeded walking quickly down the street, in her pink pompom slippers, when suddenly she felt her feet get wet, and wandered why, she looked down, and then realised she still had on her pink slippers on her feet, I need to get back, and change these wet slippers, into my leather shoes, thus, missing her train, so now she checks every time, she goes out, in case this happened again, no more embarrassing situations.

Clara pulled open her big heavy wooden door, of her old Victorian house, pulled shutting it after her, and marched quickly down the road, towards her favourite tea cafe.

She walked passed the usual red post box, past the old sweet shop, which have been opened since the nineteenth century, still selling barley sugar, and pink and white sweet mice.

Nearly colliding with children running, out of the shop, but she carried on, down the street towards The Café on the hill, before reaching the Tea Shop, Clara decided to go to the Park, before having her usual refreshments, she wanted to feel having a walk, with be an excuse to enjoy a cream tea, or date and walnut cake, which the walk giving her an appetite, for this cream tea.

Clara liked walking, and have some fresh air, and feel after having a long walk, she could muster up an appetite, for a well deserve sit down.

She came to the entrance of the Park, through the tall heavy iron gates, adorned with large iron lions, staring down at the people passing through the gates, someone must shut these gates every night, 'I am glad it is not me,' she sighed.

As she looked across at the lake, as she approached the edge of the blue still lake her first thoughts, where she wished she had brought some stale bread to feed the ducks, but never mind, I will enjoy a walk, around the lake, and maybe someone else will be feeding them, and I can watch them feed them.

On the perimeter, of the wall she came across an older man.

'Good day, Mrs Fortesque,' he remarked, lifting his hat, with this greeting.

'Oh! hello Mr hmm, trying to remember, this man's name,'

'Poor Clara, knew this man, but could not make out, where and who he was, a*s we One gets older, it does take a few minutes longer*, thought Clara.

'My name is Mr Tank,' he replied reminding Clara.

'Oh! Mr Tank, oh, hello I am sorry, but for a minute, I could not remember you, and how we met,' admitting Clara, apologising.*(He was a man, who she met on a train journey, a few years ago, he booked his seat on the train, but he sat in Clara seat, she had booked also in this seat, unfortunately Mr Tank had sat in her seat, by mistake, but she told him to stay there, I will have the seat next to yours, saving you moving He lived in the next street to Clara's and he was always passing her house frequently, now he knew she lived there.*

'Fine, replies Mr Tank I hope you do not mind me mentioning, that I see that your hedge could do with a cut, Mrs Fortesque,' he said.

'Not at all, it is rather high in places,' admitted Clara, smiling.

'May I offer you the name of my gardener, he is a godsend, so quick, kind and he cleans up, so much, I really can say that you, would not know, he has done any work.' Admitted Mr Tank.

'Funny you are mentioning this, I am looking for a gardener,' replied Clara.

'How about it when I pass your gate, I could drop his telephone number, in your letter Box,' said Mr Tank.

'Oh, how kind, thank you, what can I do for you in return, do you like puddings? I make a lot of apple crumbles, and freeze them, but I do have plenty to give,' admitted Clara.

'I do like an apple crumble, with custard,' admitted Mr Tank, with grinning.

'Really, that is my favourite too, what about you coming over on Sunday, and I can give you one from the freezer, I make apple crumble from the apples, from my tree at the back, I cook them in foil, and freeze them, you could have a frozen one, and you can thaw it out, in your fridge, why not come over this Sunday, and then you can leave me your gardener's number, and I can give you one of my frozen apples crumbles,' said Clara smiling.

'That is a deal,' said Mr Tank grinning.

CHAPTER 5

Mr Tank, left Clara to go on with her walk, he went back towards the gates, Clara carried on, as she was walking, saying that was kind of Mr Tank, smiling, kind of me too, thought Clara.

In the distance, Clara saw a man, walking towards her.

'Oh! he looks like a gypsy man, rather sunburnt thought Clara surprised to see a gypsy there. *He was wearing a jacket, baggy trousers, and a large hood, which was not on his head but dropped down on his shoulders.*

'As he walked past Clara, she noticed *in his hood a small monkey, which you sometimes see with a man, turning a musical organ, as the saying says, don't ask the monkey ask, (the organ grinder),*

I wonder if his master, has a musical organ, as soon as she said that, she came across a large portable musical organ, standing on its own by the lake.

Oh! so that is where he originally came from, where was the man going with a monkey, she turned around to see him disappear into a hut. 'Oh! what on earth is a hut for?'

Clara being a bored person, and she had plenty of time before four o'clock, decided to look closer at the hut, luckily. He did not come out, but Clara walked behind the hut, to see anything else interesting, at the back of the hut, had one window, she carefully investigated the window, and saw a man bending over a machine, and in the corner was the Monkey, sitting on a box, watching the man, the window was very dirty, so the man could not see Clara looking in, he suddenly got up, and picked up the monkey, popped him into his hood at the back of his neck, came out and locked the door and walked away. Clara was still out of site of the man, she came around the front, and found him gone, Clara walked on, and got back on the path, around the lake, as she was walking, she heard a beautiful sound, as she approached, she saw the man, with the hood, at an organ.

Oh! that is what he does, play the organs the organ, I just left just now, that is why he has a monkey, where is the monkey then, on the floor was a box, I hope he is not in that small box on the floor, eating a banana, the man had put an old hat, on the floor, hoping for some money. I will give him my change, Clara threw some coins into his hat, on the floor, and listened to the music, it was delightful, and she was so happy she clapped the man, he smiled at Clara, and said have a nice day Madam.

'Thanks,' she said, And I see that your monkey is eating a banana, well she says I have a sweet in my bag.

'Sorry miss bad for his teeth, sorry about that,' he said, apologetically.

'Oh! All right, never mind, more for me,' admitted Clara, walking on, going to the tea shop, as soon as she had enough of the Park, and the natural delights, of the surrounding of the park.

She came across a bench, and proceeded to sit down, as she looked across the lake, she gazed and said, 'what a beautiful lake.'

Clara admired the blue lake, with the occasional ripple of water gliding across the very still and peaceful waters, as she said a duck flew down gliding across the water, slowing down, just like a plane landing on an air strip, the duck was skimming across the water. Slowing down and stopping almost in front of Clara, who was amazed of this sudden arrival of a brown and black marks across his white back, on the other side of the lake a swan was swimming slowly down the lake follows by her string of cygnets, following behind her.

Clara was mesmerised with these beautiful sights, she watched the swans, and her cygnets pass by, once reaching the bank, the swan mounted the bank, followed by the string of cygnets, also mounting the bank one by one, some having difficulty getting onto the large upward climb, but the five eventually carried on following their mother, and sitting down on the grassy bank, snuggling next to their mother, which was very close to Clara, who was excited, with this spectacle she would have clapped, had it been practised and staged, whatever next she was thrilled with excitement. After the upstaged of the wild birds, she got up to go, and running in front of her was a grey squirrel which raced up a tree, then running along the branch then jumping to over another tree, and disappearing away.

Now, I really must go no more excitement, I have had enough for one day. Clara walked on towards the tea shop, she heard a child's cry, she turned around and saw a toddler in a pram crying, the child was about two years old, crying, and his mum, trying to calm him down.

'Can I be on any help?' asked Clara.

'No, thanks, he is hungry, and I need to get back to give him, something to eat. Right, maybe an apple,' asked Clara offering her apple.

The young Mum, said thanks to Clara, you don't have a dry biscuit on you, have she asks.

'No sorry, but I do have a small bar of white chocolate, in case I get hungry, I do like a bit of chocolate now and again, to keep me going, I really do not want it, I am going to The Tea shop in town, so I will not be having it, please take it,' offered Clara.

'Oh! thank you, he does like chocolate, and white chocolate does not make such a Mess,' admitted the young Mum.

Clara gets out of her bag, a bar of white chocolate,

'Here you are,' she said, handed it to her, the young mother, who unwrapped the chocolate bar, and put a small piece in the toddler's mouth, at least he cannot cry when he is eating, agreed, the young Mum.

Clara smiled, the mother smiled back.

'If you like Monkeys,' Clara thought of the Musical box (Organ grinder) on wheels, in the Park.

'Does your child like monkeys, live ones I mean, and not the soft toy sort, I have just seen a monkey in the park, with this man who is a musician, if you take him into the Park, it may take your child's mind away, from whatever he is upset about, I presume it is boy, apologise, if he is a girl, he has an outfit, with a train on the front,' mentioned Clara.

'Oh! Yes, he is boy, Mikey,' answered the young Mother.

'Thanks, what did you say a monkey, well funny you say that, he likes Monkeys, his grandfather calls him a cheeky monkey, sometimes when he plays with him, if you go through those gates, at the end of this road, you will see the park, walk about five minutes down this lane, and there by the water, is a man with a real monkey, and a few soft toy ones, on his Portable Musical box he may have one the monkey on his shoulder.

'Thanks,' said the Mother of the child, her son Mikey had

now stopped crying after Clara had arrived, it may have been Clara bright coat ,that took his mind off, but he had stopped, and started to smile, and looked like he was now enjoying being with mum. 'I will take him now, he seems much happier,' said the young Mum, thanking Clara again for kind and generosity in giving him this welcome relief from her crying child, who was making her upset and stressed, thank you very much for telling me.

She turned the pram around, and headed towards the Park gates, she turned around at Clara and smiled at Clara and waved good bye.

CHAPTER 6

Clara walked on towards the café, I will be glad to sit down, and have a cup of tea, she pushed open the door, it jangled as always, she made her way across the room to find her usual seat, the table she sat at was always, in the corner seat situated by the window, unless the sun shone through, so Clara had to move her table an inch or two, and back again, when the sun had moved away from the window. She pulled out the chair, brushing away a few crumbs, and tutting away to herself about the mess, if I sit on these crumbs it would leave greasy marks, all over my skirt, now reassured that everyone had gone from that table, and would not come back, she sat down on the chair, pulling the chair closer towards the table, shifting her skirt over her legs. Clara could now, gaze at the people coming out, of the Market place, across the road. people looking was Clara's favourite pastime, she picked up the new menu, and admiring the various contents, which may or may not tempt Clara to try something new, there was a new line up of cakes and teas, which looked like Clara might try later, she looked at the menu from cover to cover. Now let me see, she thought, putting her fingers to her lips thoughtfully. Do I have my usual tea and cake, or shall I try something different? Hmmm, not sure, Emily could have some suggestions, Auntie Bun, could have some new ingredients, in her kitchen today.

Emily, Clara familiar waitress comes over to Clara.

Good Morning Mrs Fortesque, how are you today?

Clara replied, 'very well Emily, thank you.'

How are you? asked Clara replying to Emily questions.

'Yes, thank you Mrs Fortesque, a bit of a sniffle, but apart from that fine and happy, now changing the subject, do you want your usual tea and cake?' Emily, asked she pulled out her notebook, and pencil from her white apron pocket and started to write down Clara's order.

I am sorry to hear about your sniffle, I am all geared up for the cold coming my way, I just have a hot lemon drink, and honey, that always does the trick. 'Well! Emily said Clara peeping over her glasses, still propped on her rather pointed thin nose, I see you have as always, a wonderful, array of cakes, and today I will try a slice of carrot cake, and some peppermint and orange tea, I am trying to change my image, and not be so predictable and old fashioned,' grinned Clara, who always had a good reply to Emily's suggestions.

Emily wrote Clara's order, and did not say a word, and walked back to kitchen.

Emily bought back Clara's carrot cake, she placed the carrot cake, with a cake fork, and her peppermint and orange teapot, on the table, followed by milk and sugar.

I thought you could have milk with it, all not, and a bowl of sugar.

'Thank you, Emily, Clara's looked up stared at Emily, and wondering why Emily was looking worried.

I wonder what is wrong with Emily,' Clara thoughtfully was Emily was wondering what Clara was going to do next, was she concerned with Clara's age and her ability to look after herself, or sometimes noticing the flower on her hat at the meant to be on the back of her head and not on the front.

As Clara was tucking into her tea and cakes, enjoying the

cake, and her tea, while watching the people outside, walking up and down. She was watching, several people talking in a group, with clothes fit for a wedding, in the distance was a bride, with a full gown and train, walking towards the crowds. I wonder where her groom is, oh there he is sitting in a car on the other side of the road, she looks upset. I better get on with my tea before it gets cold, she had a sip of her tea, and looks across at the shelf with leaflets on, I wonder if they are, anything going on this month, it is the month of fairs and places of interest to do, a house or a fairground, maybe that is where that Musician came from.

Clara reached over to the rack, of leaflets, while sitting down, and picking up a leaflet from the rack. She looked up and noticed a young girl staggering into the door, with a double buggy, moving backwards to open the door, as her hands were full, not to open the door was the only way she could manage it. Clara carefully put her newspaper down, and went over to the girl, to hold the door open for her.

'Oh! thank you,' said the girl thankfully.

The girl had pushed her pram, to a nearby table, with her two children, one was about two months old, and the other one look about three.

The baby of three months was asleep, and the older one was awake, and wanting a drink.

Clara looked across at the young girl, knowing what it was like having children at a café, with their food and drink, decided to help her. She grabbed a handful of serviettes, and went over to asked her, would you like these serviettes? I have to many, and I can see you have not any, and with children you always need many to wipe their faces, or mop up spills, or clean the table from messy customers on the table.

The young girl was touched by Clara kind thoughts. 'thanks you,' she murmured.

Clara was pleased to be useful, and happy she accepted them, and went back to finish her tea and cake, and she exchanged a smile with her.

The girl took out a drink for her child, and left her young one who stayed asleep, she had also ordered cake and a chocolate drink for herself, her drink was rather full, and she spilt her drink then needed a serviette to wipe it. Clara had noticed her serviette being used, and was pleased her good deed, she was gratified the need by the young girl.

Clara finished her paper, and her tea and cakes; she put out her arm and waved to Emily across the room, who was trying to remove chewing gum, from underneath a table.

Emily came back to Clara, grumbling to herself, I wish people would not put chewing gum underneath tables, as she coming to Clara, she put the chewing gum, into a paper serviette, to put it in her pocket to dispose of later.

When she came back towards Clara, her face still looked worried, like she did earlier, but she put on a brave face and smiled to Clara.

'Did you enjoy our new cake selection, and our wonderful array of teas, Mrs Fortesque? asked Emily.

'Emily, that was wonderful, I was spoilt for choice, is everything all right.

The carrot cake was delicious... I think I will need to change my outlook on life; I am stuck in my old ways and need to change. Next week I will try the oat and cinnamon slice with a caramel topping, followed by your ginger and nutmeg tea. 'I noticed you were a bit preoccupied earlier,' asked Clara, looking concerned with Emily worried expression.

This made Emily laugh, she liked old Mrs Fortesque, and her funny always she was always cheered up with Clara, saying about changing her life, and stuck in her own ways, the word stuck was reminding Emily with the chewing gum situation, she was having just then, by being firmly fixed to the table.

Emily totted up, Clara bill handing her the slip of paper.

Clara, looked at the bill, looking very pleased with the price she was asked to pay.

She got out her purse, sliding her coins into the palm of her hand, looking to make sure, she had got the right amount. She handed over the money, Emily knew that Clara was honest, just putt the whole of the coins into her large pocket of her apron.

'I will see you next week, Emily,' said Clara.

Same time Mrs Emily asked, as she went over to door, opening the door.

Bye Mrs Fortesque, smiled Emily.

'Bye Emily, and thank you, tell your ladies at the back, how wonderful their cakes and tea are, I will highly recommend it to my friends about you, Bunty and Maureen, cake, and tea, and of course you Emily, for being so sweet kind and helpful.

Thank you, Mrs Fortesque, but not all those virtues, maybe helpful. Okay, but I can always think it, and they can find out themselves when they come in.

Emily shut the door after Clara had left, and she went back to her other customers, but she also did as she is always watched Clara go home, as she did many times crossing the same road, walking back to her home.

Clara proceeded to cross the road, looking both ways, suddenly from around the corner. A bicycle came tearing down the road, crashed into Clara; she went flying onto the road.

Emily came rushing over to Clara, she had been watching Clara out of the window, Emily liked Clara her Grandmother died early, and she thought of Clara like a Grandmother, without the stress of old Grandmother to worry about.

Emily pushed the bicycle off Clara, she helped get up, as Clara got up slowly, standing up, with her arm into Clara, walking slowly back to the tea room, back on the pavement before she was crashed into, Emily pushes the door with her another unoccupied arm, pulling out a chair for Emily to sit on, you sit here Commanded Emily gently, upset that her favourite customer had been knocked down, by what she saw was a young foolish cyclist, not looking or caring who was in his way, and I will make you another cup of tea, the door jangled and the cyclist came in the tea room, he came up to Clara,

'I am terribly sorry Missy, he apology profusely, bending over Clara.

Clara was shaking, but apart from falling, she had grazed her arm slightly. 'Can I get you anything?' asked the young boy.

'No thanks,' said Clara, who was still not feeling like having a conversation with this careless young man.

The young man, went over to Emily, and slipped some money into Emily's hand for Clara, but Emily shoved it back, into the young man's hand, he quickly left the shop and picked up his bike, rushing off on his bicycle, disappearing into the town.

After Clara had her cup of tea, and Maureen came out from the kitchen, came over to give Clara a wet cloth to clean her grazed arm, Clara dried it the graze, with a clean serviette she had nearby from her laundry basket.

A gentleman nearby her table, offered to take home, which Clara did, the gentleman in question, was a neighbour eleven doors down from Clara, who offered to take her shopping, or if she needed a helping hand, he gave Clara a phone number, if she needed any help in the future, which Clara thanks and said she would if she needed him.

The following two weeks, poor Clara was hobbling around, the fall made her shaky and nervous, her arm that was grazed, Clara had cleaned it up, and put on a fresh clean plaster, which was handy, when eventually managed to go in the garden to do some light weeding, she did not want any dirt going into her poorly arm.

I think next Thursday, I will go and have my tea and cake, I miss young Emily and her smiley face.

After getting over from her fall, and her arm healing, she returned two weeks later, Clara went into the tea room as usual, she starts walking towards her seat, in the corner, but someone was already there, a large lady in her forties, with a small dog beside her, the dog barked at Clara, coming towards, which she thought she was going to go, and sit down as usual, Clara jumps, after the dog yelps at her. Clara was surprised but looked round for Emily, but another lady assistant was there, instead of Emily, Clara went over to another waitress and says. that lady is sitting in my corner seat by the window.

The waitress, said firmly to Clara, ' Miss I am not familiar with who sits where, and anywhere I do not know you, so Mrs Jackson can sit anywhere t with her Chiwawa dog, Archibald, I cannot remove her now, sorry Madam I cannot physically remove her,' she said with a big tut!

'Archibald, for a dog that is strange name to call a small dog,' said Clara, angrily.

Clara looked around to see, where else she could sit, when she sat down, she moved the other chair, also by her table, the chair made a terrible noise as Clara, scraped the floor.

Mrs Jackson look up at the noise, Clara glared across at the woman.

'The new Waitress, came over to Clara, to see what she

would like to drink,

'What has happened to Emily,' moaned Clara, shouting.

'Emily is having a baby, and she will not be back for a long time, so, you will have me to take your orders, till Emily comes back maybe next year, or whenever,' replied the waitress, who was now, getting very annoyed with Clara, for making such a fuss about Mrs Jackson, and now Emily.

'I will have cinnamon and toffee flapjack,' enquired Clara, expecting having what she liked and whenever.

'I am sorry but the lady in the corner, had the last slice of cinnamon and toffee flapjack,' said the waitress.

'Oh! That woman has now taken my cake too, this too much for me in one day, I am so annoyed, then can I have some fruit cake, last slice, hmm,' grumbled Clara, still annoyed with Mrs Jackson.

'What can I have then?' said angry Clara.

'We have scones, fruit cake, or rich biscuits, rich biscuits whatever next and some Earl Grey tea, if you got it,' grumbled Clara, feeling fed-up with this café, she thought she was happy going to but now maybe not.

'Coming up Miss,' said the waitress, trying to oblige with this horrible customer.

'I am Mrs Fortesque,' demanded Clara in a very sharp commanding voice.

The waitress brought along Clara tea and cake, putting it on the table, without a word.

Clara had her tea and fruit cake paid her the bill and stormed out of the tea room.

She was glad to leave this awful shop, with no Emily this was to much for Clara to cope with.

CHAPTER 7

After Clara's bad experience with her favourite café, she decided not to hurry going back she realised she must not get used to one person, but she has to get used to other people to take their place instead no one is irreplaceable are they. I had to get used to Michael departing from my life so losing people has made me stronger unfortunately. I must be grateful for small mercies.

I have a lovely house, I am not dependent on my family, or have any pets that rely on me, nearby I have good neighbours, who help me if I need them,' thought Clara being grateful for all she had and appreciated of them.

The following week, Clara decided to have some work done in the house. Clara rang for a builder, Mr Lewis Clara's next-door neighbour, recommended Ray Buckley, Mr Lewis, in his fifties, who is a reliable neighbour, he looked out for Clara, and his other next-door neighbour, Gilly who is slightly younger that Clara. Gilly is also alone in the world, she is always asking Mr Lewis for help with her lighting, and small plumbing jobs. Mr Lewis recommended Ray and Terry, a small builders group, from their village, they are a nice pair, reliable, tidy quick, and cheap. I like those aptitudes in a man, Mr Lewis, admitted, he likes to help his neighbours, but the bigger jobs, they a need a professional person, these builders have the right tools and knowledge.

Ray and Terry arrived at Clara's house, Ray is in his

forties, short with a paunchy stomach, and Terry, is his young apprentice, who is eighteen years old, tall and very lean.

Ray arrived, with Terry, at Clara's house, he knocked twice sharply, with the bright brass knocker, that adorned her large wooden door.

Terry, looked up at Mrs Fortesque's house, thinking he might need a long ladder to reach the roof.

'It is big house isn't it,' Mr Buckley commented Terry craning his neck, and eyeing the property' making a serious face at Ray, standing by.

' Yes,' agreed Ray, whispering in Terrys ear.

'Your missus would be lost here wouldn't she making another comment,' said Terry smiling. Ray nodded.

'Someone coming to the door,' said Terry commenting.

Quiet footsteps approached the door.

Clara came to door, Mr Buckley, I presume looking at Terry , the young apprentice.

'I'm Mr Buckley,' butted in Ray, most annoyed at this suggestion.

'Sorry you look like a Mr Buckley, I once knew 'observed Clara, smiling at an old friend , who turned out to be Terry and not him. Terry smiled to himself.

'As I said on the phone, I have several slates missing, I have a leak on the ceiling, of my kitchen, because of the slates, it was that terrible storm, we had the other day explained Clara.

'Right, no problem,' said Ray, hearing all this comment before with other customers.

Clara added 'They fell off the roof over there,' pointing to the slates on the floor.

Luckily, I was asleep.

'Nasty if they had fell on your head, or worse,' tutted Ray, sympathising with Clara.

'Leave it with us,' said Ray, heard enough and wanted to finish this job, and go home.

Ray and Terry set to work fetching the wheel barrow from the lorry with a load of slates. Terry carried the ladder over his shoulder.

An hour and a half later, they finished, Ray knocked on the back door, to tell Clara, that they had finished, and were about to pack up and go home.

'Would you like some tea and homemade cakes?' asked Clara, looking at Ray.

'Mrs Fortesque, that would be excellent,' answered Ray, smiling.

'How do you like your tea?' asked Clara.

'One sugar,' said Ray, patting his stomach must diet,' he commented.

'Two for me, I don't have a problem,' grinned Terry.

Clara held out the sugar bowl and said, help yourself.

They helped themselves to sugar. Stirring it afterwards.

'I will just get the cakes, iced ones all right,' asked Clara, happy to give her cakes to such deserving workmen.

Clara left the two men, while she got her tin of cakes, in the kitchen she put several neatly on a plate, served with a white cotton doily, she returned with cakes which were slightly burnt on top, with icing covering the top, but several were burnt.

'Sorry about the burnt ones, I went to the phone, and when I got back it was too late,' apologised Clara, looking kind of sad with her burnt offerings.

Ray laughed, my missus always burns them I call her King Albert, who burnt the cakes didn't he, but he commented about the cup of tea, he appreciated.

'Very welcome, this cuppa,' said Ray.

'Sorry about the chip, in your cup, Ray, and the crack in yours Terry, they were my best bone china, but I must give you those, so if you break them, which happens sometimes. I won't mind, and nor will you,' commented Clara.

'No, Mrs Fortesque, we understand, my missus does the same, she is fussy over her cups too, when we have plumbers in, they have the old cups too.' he admitted scratching his head.

'I will not be around next week,' replied Ray, we have a big conversion in a shop.

'We will probably be a week or two doing this job, so if you need us, we can come back in a months' time, Mrs Fortesque,' Clara admitted to them.

'Your prices are far high for me to afford you again, but thanks for warning me anyway,' said Clara, gathering the cups and plates of cakes, with two biscuits, left on the plate.

'I will send you a bill next week, when I have worked out our costs,' said Ray.

'I hope the bill will be fair,' asked Clara, anxiously.

'We do our best to give our customers a fair price, seeing you gave us a cuppa and your lovely cakes, we may deduct some off the bill, we charge higher, if they do not give us cakes, commented Ray grinning.

'Oh, thank you, I do like to spoil people if I can,' admitted Clara.

Ray and Terry left Clara, and drove off, with the dusty lorry roaring down the road.

Clara had to stay in her house for a week with a nasty cold, when Clara was Better,

I must go out and do some shopping, and get my cup of tea from The Hill top cafe, although I miss Emily, I do hope that large lady is not there with her yappy dog, shall I go on Sunday Clara thought, she was still wondering if she should go out on Monday and do some shopping I am getting short of milk and bread.

When she was thinking about going out, she heard a knock at the door, I am not expecting anyone today, Clara goes to the window, to check who was at the door, she could just see a foot, the rest of the person was hidden, she craned her neck to see if she could see this person, this person moves slightly, oh know I see who it is Mr Tuck, he did say he was coming Clara opens the door.

'Hello! Mr Tank,' said Clara, surprised with him arriving and not warning her.

I have the name of my gardener, you said you needed to do your hedge

'Oh! thanks,' said Clara taking the note with the address written on it, from Mr Tanks Hand.

Clara looks at the name, she squinted to try to read this scribbled down name on the tiny piece of paper.

Oh, is it Ralph Peppers, trying to read Mr Tanks handwriting.

'Yes, that right, he lives around the corner, in the end terrace house with Horace the cat.

Oh! smiled Clara, smiling at a big name for a cat.

Horace is very old tabby, to finish all details of the conversation.

'Now come in, Mr Tank, remember I said you could have one of my apples crumbles, I just happened to thaw one out, in case if you came, you could have it today, or I will have it for tea, if is almost thawed, but not till tomorrow, which will be just cold enough to reheat, please come in, and I can give it to you if you want to take it home,' said Clara obliging.

Mr Tank follows Clara, into the kitchen.

'Do want to sit on this chair?' asked Clara, pulling out a chair for Mr Tank.

'Yes! thank you, Clara, if I may,' asked Mr Tank, sitting down on the chair that Clara pulled out for him.

'Would you like a cup of tea, I have just put the kettle on,' asked Clara.

'Thank you, it would be so appreciated, or a glass of water,' said Mr Tank.

'I am very thirsty, too, after having a salty bacon breakfast today,' remarks Clara,

'Yes,' admits Mr Tank, my soup too was salty, I must have put in too much salt.

'Oh! how awful, you really must be thirsty,' sympathised Clara, with in his dry Mouth.

'I am guilty of that too much salt, food needs salt to enjoy, I should put in pepper, but I manage without it, but I am a lover of salad cream, and tomato sauce,' admits Clara.

'Me too, agreed, Mr Tank...'

'Now the kettle has boiled I will make the tea, how do you like your tea?' Mr Tank asks Clara...

'Weak ten, please Mrs Fortesque,' admitted Mr Tank.

'Fine I will brew it, and then you can have the first pour,' said Clara, pleased to know what Mr Tank required.

Clara poured the water, and two teaspoons of tea, into the tea pot, and waited, in the meanwhile she got out her best tea service, and put two saucers, and two cups, the pattern on the cups were violets and the greenery.

'They are pretty,' remarks Mr Tank.

'Yes, a present from my husband on our wedding

anniversary, china, oh yes and I think that paper is for the first, my dear husband was very good on remembering anniversaries, always gave the right presents such a dear,' said Clara wiping a tear from her eyes.

'Oh, I am sorry I made you sad,' said Mr Tank,

No problem, I often have a tear when I think of my dear husband, Michael, now let's get this tea poured, Clara got the milk out of the fridge, and pours out milk into the cups.

'Here you are,' said Clara, giving Mr Tank a cup of tea.

'Thanks,' said Mr Tank, having a sip of tea.

'Now that cup of tea was very pleasant, and thank you for the apple crumble,' commented Mr Tank, very pleased with his gift of this pudding.

'Not at all, I am glad you like apple crumbles,' admitted Clara.

'I must get going, I have several jobs that need doing today, and I have elderly friend coming to see me this afternoon, she is bringing a tea pot over, she dropped it on the floor, and the handle has a slight chip, and I said if she brought it over, I would mend it for her,' said Mr Tank.

'Yes, me too,' said Clara.

Mr Tank got up, and went to the door, Clara opened the door, for him.

He turned around to Clara.

Thank you, Clara, he grinned, and walked down the path, opening the gate, and disappearing down the road.

Clara shut the door, and sat down on a chair, and fell asleep.

CHAPTER 8

Today is the day Clara changes the bedsheets from her bed, she is just putting on the clean sheets on her bed, and nearing the finishing touches to the bed by tucking the sheet down under the mattress.

Clara heard a knock on the door, she announced 'It sounds like a person that is desperate for my attention, I must see who it is, I hope it isn't anyone I don't want to see.' moaned Clara.

Thinking out loud, 'Last week a woman came to the door, it was a Gypsy woman standing there hoping to sell me her bunches of Lavender sprays, and she also had a large basket of odds and all sorts, offering me wooden buttons, blue ribbons, wooden homemade clothes pegs, metal lucky charms and trinkets, and well her beautiful bunches of Lavender all tied up with a dainty blue satin ribbon, I could not resist these lavenders from her, knowing the smell of lavenders were divine, and it was something to buy and keep this gypsy happy and maybe leave me alone, I thought that lavender was a deterrent to keep flies or wasps away from my kitchen. I had forgotten I already have my own lavender bushes in the garden somewhere at the end of the garden hidden near other bushes. Away I will have to try it and see, if it works in my kitchen, or was it something else, anything to keep those pesky flies off my food. I was amazed with her after I paid her the appropriate cost of the two bunches, she repeatedly thanked me, and said with a predication, that soon your luck will change, and happiness will come forth to you, and with that she left me, with these surprised predictions.'

Clara looked out of the window this time, to make sure who it was, but luckily it wasn't a gypsy coming back with more wares in her basket. No, thank goodness, it wasn't, it looks like my neighbour from up the road. Whatever does she want, thought Clara, slightly annoyed at this disruption of her finishing her bed making. In fact, she looks very upset about something, I better go downstairs and see what she wants.

The time she eventually getting to the door, it was Clara's steep stairs, and the length of them made her take longer than that in most houses getting to the door, some callers were impatient with waiting for Clara to appear I do not understand some houses have long stairs than most she thought.

Clara was right her neighbour did look upset, she was standing there, looking very distressed.

Evelyn, Clara's neighbour, was there but not keeping still with waiting, was very impatient for the door to open.

'Evelyn, how are you?' Asked Clara. Smiling and hoping for one back, but hoping she was okay anyway.

She did look very worn and tired, with dark rims under her eyes, dressed in a brown grubby coat, and beside her on the step with her a small suitcase.

Evelyn, conveyed to Clara, 'Can I stay here for one night please?' she begged her.

'Yes! of course, you can, you can stay two or three nights it you want to, I am not fussed to how long you stay, but why what is wrong, you look so… upset. What has happened?' Clara wanted to know why and curious that she was so upset to come to her house, when she rarely saw her appear out of her house, except on Market day on occasion.

Evelyn was a single lady, never married and kept herself to herself, but today she was out, asking for help.

Evelyn told Clara she has new neighbours who have just arrived and moved next door, and they have decided to knock down walls and do lots of DIY jobs, and generally make a noise morning, noon and night, 'So my sleep has been interrupted for several days, and I am at my wits end, exhausted, tired, and depressed, the smell from the chemicals they also use, is horrible the stuff they throw out in their garden is just rubbish and nasty. I just want one good night sleep, but if you are busy then I will go back home and endure the noise, and use my ear plugs, but the noise still vibrates through them, although the earplugs shut off some noise, when I go to the bathroom, my ear plugs in my ears drop out on the floor, and sometimes fall between the slacks between the banister rail. I cannot bend down, in case I fall down the stairs retrieving them.' admitted Evelyn sighing.

'Yes, yes, of course you can stay here, come in, come in.' repeated Clara, getting more stressed with Evelyn, more than her, with her stress, and the ranting from her about the builders.

Evelyn steps inside, leaving her suitcase on the doorstep. Clara reminds Evelyn about her suitcase.

'Is that your suitcase, Evelyn?' asked Clara, pointing to it.

'Oh yes, I nearly forgot it, the stress has made me forget what I am doing.' she said quickly.

Clara admitted she was upstairs making the bed, 'But now you are here I will do it later. I need a cup of tea anyway. Go and sit in the lounge, while I put the kettle on to make us a cup of tea.' ordered Clara 'I think you need something stronger or am I wrong?' Clara asked, she was hoping she said she could which would relax her and stop her feeling so stressed out.

'Yes, I would like something stronger, but I do not drink alcohol.' she muttered.

'Not a problem, tea it will be.' admitted Clara realised that alcohol was not the answer to this or any other problem, but she did not know why she wanted her to drink alcohol, which would make her drunk and disorderly maybe?

Evelyn came gingerly in, looking around the house nervously, she had never been in this house before and wasn't a one to go and socialise easily. Evelyn looked up and noticed on the wall a painting and was also amazed at a certain oil painting there.

'I love your painting of you got on the wall, it is your portrait.' asked Evelyn, admiring this portrait of Clara smiling in the picture.

'Yes, my dear husband Michael had it commissioned for me, so if I went first, he would always know I was there looking down at him looking after him, but unfortunately he went first, so but luckily, I only have a photograph of him, alas no oil painting. Now more of morbid talk lets go and have this cup of tea and a choccy biscuit.' announced Clara smiling.

'Can I help you get the teacups?' Evelyn asked nervously.

'No, I am fine thanks, go into my lounge through there, pointing to a door, on the table, there is a magazine from St Mathews Church, if you would like to read it while I am making the tea that would be a help.' announced Clara.

Evelyn smiled, and left Clara heading towards the kitchen.

Evelyn went through the lounge door and walked in, she felt strange being there, she was not a person who made friends easily. Clara's house had a dusty smell about it, but nice, warm friendly with a good feeling about it, she felt at home there. Evelyn thought she would look out of the window, and went towards the large window, and peered outside, to witness Clara's garden.

Clara's garden was something that only some people who were there could see, people outside never saw the garden, or her neighbours from their house windows, that she had a secret garden...

Evelyn was enjoying Clara's house which was calm, peaceful, and quiet, with a lovely view from her Victorian window which was extremely comforting, then the noise from the banging on the walls from her neighbour, now Evelyn appreciated the solitude and sanctuary of the house, as she was feeling secure and very well protected.

Evelyn looked around for this magazine that Clara had mentioned earlier she spotted the magazine on the coffee table and sat down on an armchair feeling very relaxed on the soft cushion on here, she started flipping through the pages, and getting completely absorbed with all the articles in there.

Clara eventually came in with a trayful of tea and biscuits. Smiling with the knowledge that Evelyn was now looking much more relaxed than she did earlier.

She carefully put the tray down on the table and sat herself down on a large cushion seat from her comfy sofa.

Evelyn had her head buried down in her magazine, not hearing anything or anyone, but enjoying having this lovely quiet lady giving her a bed and now a cup of tea, with chocolate biscuits.

Evelyn looked up from the noise of teapot pouring from Clara silver teapot out into her cup made her aware that Clara was there, with her best silver tea service.

Clara, being well-to-do and knowledgeable about doing the right thing, always put the tea in the cup first, as they do in certain upper-class households, with the milk poured in afterwards.

'How are you enjoying the magazine?' asked Clara putting down the tea pot while asking.

'Yes, thank you.' and she buried her head again, obviously needing to read more, knowing once she left the house, she will not be able to read it again.

'Are you enjoying reading it?' asks Clara, interested but never read it before, but always felt guilty if she threw away anyway,

Evelyn answered, 'Everything in there, the silly jokes, and articles about the WI, and their meetings, and they also mentioned they need bell ringers to volunteer to ring on Sundays at their church.'

'Oh nice.' said Clara not wishing to participate in heavy bell ringing.

Clara visits the Church, she isn't a churchgoer, but went to talk to the Vicar on occasions, as the Vicar was very kind to her when she lost her Michael recently.

'I used to go to church as a child,' admitted Evelyn 'We had to go, as Mother shooed us out of the house to get on with the Sunday roast.'

'My parents were not churchgoers,' admitted Clara 'They thought it was a waste of time, when they had work the next day, but saying that, they were extremely generous people, always giving money to charities, kind and very good to strangers, never galivanting or leaving us on our alone. My mother cooked cakes when we came home, we were starving and very thirsty, we were, very lucky my brother and me we were given mother's homemade cakes and a drink of lemonade.' smiled Clara.

'I have a sister and two brothers,' said Evelyn 'Good boys they both are, one a monk and works in Scotland, and the brother works with children in a children's home being a house father, with another lady who is the house mother, and my sister is married to a farmer on Exmoor.'

'Very nice,' now Clara changed the subject 'How many lumps, Evelyn?' asks Clara, picking up the silver tongs.

'Two lumps please.' said Evelyn smiling.

Clara picked up two lumps of sugar from her silver sugar bowl, dropping them into Evelyn cup, which splashed the tea cloth with dropping them in Evelyn cup of tea. Clara handed her the cup of tea, with Evelyn reached over to taking hold of the cup.

Now Evelyn sat back on her armchair, relaxed and happy in the knowledge of some peace and quiet from her house, which she had endured so long.

Clara offered Evelyn a biscuit from a plate of biscuits containing garibaldi, pink wafers, and plain rich tea biscuits. Evelyn took a garibaldi biscuit, looking at Clara, knowing cheeky name for this biscuit that wasn't garibaldi.

Clara gave Evelyn a plate to put her biscuit on, later than she should have done.

They both drank their tea in silence. Clara was glad of this excuse to sit and relax too, having been busy with her chores that morning and the afternoon, with only Evelyn's interruption. which she was a glad of so she could have a well-deserved cup of tea and a biscuit. She could have offered Evelyn a piece of cake, but Clara had the last one yesterday for her afternoon tea in the garden, when she thought she deserved a piece of cake after a hard graft of cutting a big branch from an apple tree. She hoped she had cut it right, with no disease to set in, without putting any proper.

Evelyn finished her tea, putting the cup back on the table, ignoring Clara, and carrying on reading at the Church News magazine.

Clara did want to talk either, she just sipped her hot cup of tea, as she hadn't put enough milk in her tea to cool it down.

Evelyn blue eyes started to droop, and luckily as she had no cup on her lap, sat back in her chair and she slowly went to sleep.

Clara had noticed Evelyn falling asleep, she had already finished her tea, she thought this would be a good idea to go upstairs and finish making her bed and make up one for Evelyn too.

As she got, she heard Evelyn, snoring loudly, much to Clara relief that she was well and truly asleep and relaxed and she would be asleep for at least another half an hour or more, so that Clara could finish what she was doing to her bed making before she was interrupted earlier.

Clara tiptoed out of the room and went upstairs to her bedroom.

She eventually finished the bed making sure they were all tucked in with all the sheets in the appropriate places and went across to the airing cupboard to find some suitable bed sheets for Evelyn.

This will do nicely, she thought, getting some fresh sheets, and smelling them to make sure. Hmm, nice and fresh, perfect for Evelyn.

Clara took them across to the boudoir, which is the guest room for Evelyn. She went back to the airing cupboard and got out two warm blankets, one blue and one coloured one. I have not been in the boudoir since Auntie Katie came over to stay, before she boarded on her plane carrying her way on her way to Australia to see her family, and thinking about her, she was happy here, that she said the hot water bottle I gave her in bed was perfect for my cold toes, Auntie Katie had admitted. I must call her someday; over there it is not too expensive to call in our mornings.

Clara promptly went over to the window unlatching the hook and moved it upwards thus opening it, and letting in the lovely breeze from outside, and noticing that the sill had a grey layer of dust along it, as she had not visited this room for a long time.

'Oh, this is dusty,' she said rubbing her finger along the sill 'I must get a cloth sometime and give it a clean.'

Clara went back to the bed, adding the blankets. She had then finished it and stood back to admire her nicely made bed.

As she did, she felt someone coming into the room, behind her. It must be Evelyn, she thought turning around, she expected Evelyn to say something about her sleeping arrangements.

'Evelyn, you are awake now, I never expected.' she started to say, but there was no one there, 'Never mind, must be my tiredness causing these strange thoughts.' admitted Clara, feeling maybe I am more overtired with the house and garden work than I thought.

Clara left the room and went back downstairs to find Evelyn still asleep.

She was still asleep, and not upstairs in the boudoir, never mind, now she is asleep I need to decide what to eat, now there are two of us to consider for food, thought Clara.

She went into the kitchen to carry on with making a meal.

Clara did not feel alone, for a change, just felt someone was around, this may her thought that she felt that Evelyn gave her this feeling being in the lounge with a sense of she had company.

When Clara had finished the preparation, she went back to sit waiting for Evelyn to stir.

Whilst it was quiet, in the background all of a sudden Clara heard a loud bang noise from upstairs, and thought nothing of it, probably a door slamming from the wind of the window in the boudoir upstairs that she had opened earlier, giving the room some airing before she slept there.

The mantlepiece clock in Clara lounge suddenly struck six o clock, thus waking up Evelyn who eyes slowly opened and was slowly aware she was not at home but in Clara's house.

'Oh, hello!' said Evelyn, looking slightly embarrassed at dropping off in someone else's house.

She rubbed her eyes and started come to from her much-refreshed sleep.

'Hello,' said Clara glad to see her awake to give her something to eat and spend the evening with her to see what else she needed to get her back happy into her house again.

'I have made your bed Evelyn, you are in my boudoir room, it has a nice view and it is at the back of the house, very quiet and peaceful you should have a good night sleep there.' admitted Clara.

'Oh, thank you.' said Evelyn thankful she was in good company away from the racket of her neighbour's noise.

Clara and Evelyn had a good first meal of stew and vegetables, followed by Clara's homemade plum tart, with hot creamy custard. Clara enjoyed this sudden intrusion of Evelyn, she was happy to help someone, and to help someone in dire straits in need of a sanctuary to go to, they had a good chat together, talking about this and that, with Clara making a hot milky cocoa drink a chocolate digestive with it. The clock struck eleven o'clock, and Clara said to Evelyn 'I must be going to be soon. What time do you normally go?' asked Clara.

'Well, half past ten normally, unless I fall asleep on the sofa, then later.'

'I will show you where your bedroom is, the bathroom and any other requirements you need. Did you did bring a toothbrush and toothpaste?' asked Clara, as Clara picked up Evelyn's suitcase.

'I have everything but toothpaste, with the rush of everything I forgot.' informed Evelyn.

'In the bathroom is my toothpaste, you can have that one, it is peppermint one, with the blue top, make sure it is toothpaste and not hand cream, they both look the same.' informs Clara.

'Thank you, Clara, you are an angel.' admitted Evelyn.

Clara said nothing, but smiled at her, relieved to be away from Evelyn sorrows, but walked towards the stairs with Evelyn close behind.

They reached the boudoir, and went in, Evelyn whispered 'It is lovely bedroom, better that a four-star hotel.' admitted Evelyn, excited at a free room.

Evelyn went over to the window and opened it, as she found it shut, and Clara's garden had a reason to open it, she threw her clothes on a nearby chair, she wasn't bothered about tidy clothes in the morning just wanting a quiet and peaceful nights sleep, thankful for not woken by noisy neighbours next door.

Clara left Evelyn alone and went to her bedroom for a good sleep and have the time to herself again.

Next morning Clara was downstairs preparing breakfast.

Evelyn came into the kitchen.

'Hello Evelyn, did you sleep well.' asked Clara kindly.

'Yes and no.' she said.

'Yes and no, sorry what do you mean?' asked Clara puzzled at her yes and no question.

'I was fast asleep, and I heard you come into my bedroom,' she said 'You woke me up.' she said slightly annoyed at Clara's interruption.

'Did you say I woke you up?' implied Clara slightly startled with her assumption.

'Yes! did you come in and shut my window, I opened it before I went to sleep hoping for some fresh air, which was nice as my bedroom window at home was shut tight because of the noise of the neighbours so I thought it would be lovely having the air from it , the bang of the window was so loud it woke me up, I saw you walk back towards the door. I went back to sleep, but why did you come in then, I could have shut it before I went to sleep without waking me.' she said crossly, adding 'You then switched on my light, and then off again, but in the morning, you kindly ironed and folded my clothes, then you lay them on the back of the chair, ready for me this morning.' she said smiling with gratitude.

'Sorry did you say I came into your bedroom?' asked a puzzled Clara 'Your window was open before I left the room yesterday, I too like the window open at night, so, I opened it before shutting your door. I am positive it was open when I finished making your bed, I have not idea about your clothes or shutting your window or putting the lights on and off, it does look like someone else did it for you, but it wasn't me.' admitted Clara upset with this accusation.

'No, I opened it before I went to sleep.' admitted Evelyn.

'I opened it,' said Clara repeating herself 'But I did NOT come into your room last night, in fact I sleep soundly and did not wake at all.'

'Oh. Then who did then?' asked Evelyn.

'Yesterday I had the same problem, I was her in your room, and I felt you behind me, but there was no one there, so this is a puzzle too.' said Clara.

'Oh! Could it be a...' said Evelyn.

'You mean a...' said Clara.

'Yes.' said Evelyn.

'Let's forget this and get breakfast.' said Clara.

'Yes, lets I am starving.' admitted Evelyn.

'Good, me too.' admitted Clara.

'Clara, I loved being here despite the window problem last night, you were very kind to me, in my time of trouble and need, but I do need to go back to the house, I have the milk man coming in this morning and he may get worried if I do not take in the milk, later that day if I failed to bring in the milk later, he would be knocking on every door to find out what happened to me, so that I must do, for my neighbours too, if my curtains are shut, they may also worry, and I feel after the sleep in the afternoon in your lovely warm lounge, and the few hours last night I feel strong enough to face the noise again.'

'But if you want to come again if the same thing happened again, you could come back, but surely the noise will eventually stop, they cannot knock walls forever, can they?'

'No, you are right they will stop, anyway thank you again, I will let you know if I hear any more noises.'

'No of course Evelyn, it is nice to have company, come again if you have any more disruptions to your sleep, this house is normally quiet, but obviously not last night, it maybe a one off happening.'

'In fact, Clara, this is not the first time this has happens to me but will try and ignore this problem!'

Clara was very aware of this happening to some people but brushed it off as normal in some circles of life.

After a good breakfast and Evelyn staying for coffee, finally Evelyn left Clara, and went back home.

Two weeks later the phone rang, and Evelyn conveyed to Clara that 'The builders had left the next day after I came back, I had a lovely time with you Clara, when the builders went the following day an elderly couple moved in, eventually speaking to me over the wall, and they are said that it was their son and daughter that bought their house, and did up for them to move in, and they apologised for the noise from the walls being knocked down and other noises there. The elderly couple came over and gave me a lovely cake, made by her daughter, who had a new cake shop in town, the cake was delicious, from her own shop, a Victorian cake with her homemade raspberry jam, inside it.'

Clara was relieved to hear good news about Evelyn's house, and her lovely new neighbours!

Clara never heard any more from the strange noises in the house or felt any presence of that thing after Evelyn left. The house felt quiet still, with a feeling of calm, peace, and tranquillity once again.

Clara felt ready to help the next poor soul who needed her help, but for now Clara is planning a trip to either the large town closer to her village, or the city one further away, this is something that needs thinking about, an early morning city centre trip, or a local town, with a slower pace in the morning to travel on a bus, she possibly would like a train trip, with an making an early start, and treat herself to those tall departmental buildings with several floors, that have clothes and bed on different floors, and a lovely restaurant for her lunch time meal, with a hot milky chocolate drink covered in grated chocolate!

CHAPTER 9

Clara, always looked forward to her usual Thursday treat at her favourite café, I have missed this because of my nasty cold, now I am better, I expect Emily has missed me, as much as I have missed her, it is a shame, I never invited her over, so I could give her a cup of my tea, and wait on her for a change, never mind there is always another time, anyway I nearly here, and I hope Emily is here too, so I can catch on her news, if she has any.

'Ah ha! here I am at Sunnydale Close, this is where the tea shop is,' Clara said to herself.

Clara walked towards her café, she stopped in her tracks.

'Oh! what is this, this looks different, what has happened to our, no, no my Tea Shop, where is my tea shop,' Clara, gasped with horror, sounding very upset and shocked, to see her Tea café no longer there, I have not been away, but not that long, sighed Clara. This is worrying, what has happened to the old ladies, who runs it, and little Emily, no Emily, this is a total nightmare, when will I ever see my Emily again!

This shop looks like a hairdresser, by reading the half-spelt spelling, on the top of the café, SALLYANN HAI, reading it out loud, yes, it sounds like a Hairdressers salon name, Clara looked around the area, just to make sure she was in the right place, and wasn't in another street, she looked across at the street name, it was definitely Sunnydale Close, that is where it was, but oh well, must be the right place then, Clara spotted a ladder, with a man, at the top of it painting the letter R of the word, HAIR.

Clara watched him painting the sign, he was busy painting away, when he shouted down to Clara, seeing that she was very old, and may not be not aware of this ladder, and she could bump into it, or stumble over it, thinking Clara could push him off the ladder by mistake, shouted down to her. 'Mine the ladder missus,' he was worried she would knock his ladder and send him flying down on the hard pavement below.

'Thanks,' said Clara, gratefully, she promptly walked around the ladder, just as well she did not know what he may be thinking about Clara being clumsy and doddery. There was another man, at the bottom of the ladder, holding the ladder steady making sure, that the Salon customers did not get paint on their heads, before having their hair done!

Clara was not having any more doubts, to where her tea shop had gone, she decided to investigate this mystery, she pushed the door open, stepping inside, she spotted, a few women milling around, cleaning and generally sweeping and cleaning the shop, in the corner Terry was putting up shelf, and Ray was putting a sink in the corner, those are the two men, who came to mend my roof the other day, she whispered to herself.

A pretty woman, with overall on came over to Clara, *who was looking around the shop in amazement at the transformation going on.*

'Hello Madam, we are currently closed now for business,' said the lady, who was cleaning the mirrors on the wall.

'I am wondering where the tea shop is, I come here regularly, every Thursday, but I have been away nursing a cold, so I wasn't told about this happening,' explained Clara was still in shock not able to see Emily anymore.

'It is not here any more madam, it is now a new hair salon, we have taken over from Maureen and Bunty,' she explained.

Clara looked around, hoping she was in a bad dream, and Emily would appear with a menu, but no, this is a new shop converted into a hairdresser so different pictures on the walls were replaced by mirrors, and hairstyle pictures too.

'Sorry about this Miss,' sadly said the lady cleaning the mirror.

'I am Mrs Fortesque,' replied Clara, angry and sad with this shocking news.

Mrs Fortesque would you like your hair done, we are slightly cheaper, than the other hairdressers in the area now we are giving complimentary price for three months so people can come to see if we are better than our competitors and cheaper than Mary Louise, up the road.

Clara knew her hair needed washing soon, since she was ill, she had not washed it for two weeks. She bent down to look at herself in the mirror.

She had calmed down, and stop being angry, with this shock of the changeover maybe it does need a wash and cut now I have noticed, it needs to be done soon.

'When are you going to be open?' Clara asked, now got used to the tea shop had gone for good, and no longer come back, with her sweet and little Emily, she would must find another tea shop, next week. 'I never know, I may find a hairdresser closing, and they might have a tea shop opening instead,' laughed Clara at her own jokes. Maybe she could use this hairdresser, and would be a new Clara immerging from here, strange she said this to Emily, and now it has happened in the same shop. As she was telling Emily, when she was commenting, she wanted to change her image.

We are opening next week, and if you want an appointment, or would you like our new appointment cards, with the telephone number on, then you can call us, saving you a journey, into town.

See that the lady, over on the older side, the one with the black overalls on, by the desk, she will give you a business card, with all our details on.

'Clara, thanked the lady and went over to the lady by the desk,' she explained, that she would like a business card, with your details on, so I can ring you up next week, explained Clara to her, she picked up a card from a box of cards, and handed Clara a card.

Clara looks at the card, reading it to herself.

'Lovely,' she commented, a beautiful picture on the front of the card, I do like your printed words, beautiful handwritten words, with a nice style, very chic.

'Yes, thank you, Madam, our model is my granddaughter,' explained the women with a broad smile on her face.

'Nice,' commented Clara, tucking the card into her large pocket on her coat.

Clara, left the shop and decided to treat herself to a bar of chocolate and newspaper.

She glanced at herself in a nearby shop, and saw that she looked rather tired, and her hair looked very messy, so she decided not to go to the shop, for a chocolate bar and paper, but to go straight home, and do some gardening instead.

Clara came home, and sat down, and made herself a cup of tea, before heading back out into the garden.

The next week, on the Monday, Clara rang up for appointment, as she rather not goes out till her hair was washed and set again , she was really embarrassed, that her hair is such a mess.

Clara was busy for the next week, doing the garden, but she managed to do her hair wash later on, after her gardening. But it will be nice to have a proper wash and cut, she admitted to herself.

Eventually Tuesday arrived, and Clara went along for her appointment, she had realised to herself, that the tea shop had gone, and she needed to investigate to see what else was around, to take the place of her lovely tea shop.

Clara went along to Sally Ann hairdressers salon, she looked up at the sign, just to make sure that she was at the hairdressers shop, yes, it is now a Sally Ann's hairdresser.

Clara walked in to the salon, and went over to the desk, looking around at the Walks admiring the new salon, with pictures of beautiful ladies, with their modern hair styles adorned on the walls.

At the desk a young woman was busy, with her head bent over the appointment book, writing down an enquiring note, and with the other hand holding the phone,

She looked up, and asked Clara, ' hello! can I help you,

'Yes! I have an appointment,' says Clara, interested to see her.

Hold on a minute, Madam, while I just write down this lady's appointment in the book.

She jotted down the appointment down, in her appointment book, then closed the book, and spoke to the lady on the phone, about the time, and the hairdresser she will must do her hair, saying goodbye, she put the phone back down,

Then coming back to Clara.

Clara, was noticing that the lady looked familiar, she could not stop and stare at the young girl at the desk.

'You do look familiar, in fact you look like a girl named Emily,' explained Clara, rather pleased and puzzled at the likeness,

'Did she work at the tea shop, this Emily?' asked the young girl.

'Yes,' said Clara grinning.

'That is my twin sister,' she said smiling, at this Clara who knew Emily.

'My name is Emma,' announced said Emma holding out her hand for Clara, to shake.

Clara shook Emma hand, saying, 'pleased to meet you, so what happened to Emily then, where is she now?' asked, Clara excitedly.

Emma explained, 'Emily had a baby, and decided to get married to Gary, she met him in the café, he often came in the café, with his Mother for tea, one day, it was his Mother's birthday, so they asked Maureen and Bunty to make her a cake, and Emily was the waitress that day, so she bought it over to the table, and this is where they met, after his mother's birthday celebrations, after that Gary, came over to have his tea, this time alone, he was very generous, he always gave Emily large tips, and Emily was very happy with his tips he, always gave her, eventually he asked Emily out, on her birthday, he found out when she had her birthday, which was on the July the twenty second, she was reluctant to tell him, knowing he may buy her a present, but he did not give her a birthday present, instead he gave her the day before her birthday an engagement ring.

The day before her birthday, he came in for his usual tea, and tea cakes, and in front of all the customers, Gary, asked Emily to marry him!

The customers had heard what was happening, waiting for her answer, the café when very quiet, little did Emily realise, that the café customers had heard this announcement from Gary Emily quietly thought about it then said YES PLEASE! the whole of the café clapped and cheered, at the announcement, and Bunty and Maureen came out carrying a lovely iced cake with the words on CONGRATULATIONS ON in Pink icing written across it.

Emily was flabbergasted, she was laughing and crying at the same time, with happiness.

After that day, things changed, Emily left, the café lost it Emily, and the hubbub of the café, Maureen and Bunty missed Emily, and decided they would retire.

Bunty had a problem with her feet, standing all day doing all the cooking, did not help, so they decided the two of them would, go down to Devon and enjoy the cream teas down there, and maybe when they could, help another café with some help with their knowledge of cakes and bread, we miss Emily she has left the district with Basil, Basil mother died, and left Basil the house, as he had not siblings to share it with.

They sold that house, and bought a house in the North west, they are hoping for a large family. Emily would like to run a B and B, or a small hotel one day, with her knowledge of waitressing, she knew what people like, she is not afraid of hard work, and Gary worked in Hotel, in the receptionist/ bar work in the evenings.

That is Emily's story now I will get your hair done for you. Mrs Fortesque, you will look amazing and happy, with your hair being done today. This salon has had top training, with the famous hairstylist. In London, do you remember Mr Wheatley the famous hairstylist, who started the wave cut? He taught my

Employer all about layers and waves, even making straight hair, with a good wave in it.

Clara was happy, to see someone, who looked familiar Emma looked at the appointment book for Clara's name.

Clara, why don't you sit and wait here for your turn, while you are waiting for your turn, would you like tea or coffee, tea please, biscuits or a cake,

'Cake, please piped up,' Clara.

'Well, it was my auntie Liz, that supplied the cakes for the cafe, occasionally, when Bunty and Maureen were on holiday sometimes, once every three months, when they needed a break from the kitchen, she was very good, I think as good as Bunty and Maureen, but now she is redundant, she is now making cakes, for this shop too.

'Really!' smiled Clara, pleased with hearing her cakes had not completely gone for good.

'Which cake are your favourite?' asked Emma.

'Oat cake, topped with cinnamon icing, and tea, with peppermint if you have it,' said Clara feeling happy now She can have her cake and eat it!

'Well!' said Emma.

Here is the list we have, we do like to keep out customers happy, handing Clara a list of cakes and teas on a menu.

I heard that you knew the café Mrs Fortesque, piped up Frances, Clara looked to see where this voice was coming from, a lady, with permed grey hair, a pink jumper and black and white skirt came over to Clara.

I run this hair salon now, with Maureen's cousin Michelle, the lady who ran the tea shop, who has gone to Devon, with Bunty.

'Emma bought over Clara's tea and cake,' Clara said.

'Now, I will never miss my teashop, because it is all here, nice people, nice premises, and then my hair done by lovely Patsy, who spoilt me now, I am having my hair done, with a lovely tea and cakes how perfect.

Clara went home completely satisfied with Emily to where she was and not disappeared. But happy with her new life.

Now settled with her beautiful hair do, Clara hoped to be carried, on with her normal life, making jams and any other cooking requirements that are needed to be done for her friends or anyone who wants them.

CHAPTER 10

After her new hairdo on Thursday, the very next morning Clara woke up feeling very positive about today, in fact I feel I would like to put on my favourite yellow hat with flowers on.

Is this going to be a good day for a hat? As long as the wind is calm, and the sun is shining this will be fine, other days, No! Now let me see... (with her thoughtful face, leaning her hand on her face as she was thinking) The flowers on my hat I have not noticed before have a different meaning, I do know some means friendship or something like that. I need to find my flower meaning book. The one a great Aunt gave mum for her birthday, which Mum gave me ten years ago as she had no more use of it.

'Now! where is it? Hmm, of course, the bookshelf, silly me,' said Clara to herself.

She reached the lounge and walked across to the book shelf which was stacked high up with her own books and that of her parents, which she received from them when clearing their house many years ago after they had to go into a home, as both of them were unable to manage together and Clara, being many miles away from them, preferred to be together in a home than being with Clara who had a stair, and could only offer one room as she had her husband and children still living at home.

Clara moves several books to find the right one. Eventually she found it, at the end of the shelf, Flowers And their Meaning in beautiful photographic pictures by Adriene Matlock.

'Oh! good here it is,' she gasps.

She pulled out the book and look through it to make sure that it was the one.

'Lovely just what I want,' she exclaimed.

Clara finds herself a nice comfy chair and makes herself comfortable to enjoy reading this colourful and beautiful book with clear pictures of flowers. She flips through the pages absorbing the beautiful illustrations of the whole book.

'Oh, I need the hat to make sure all these flowers are here; I should have brought it with me with me, ah dear,' she sighs.

Clara gets up and goes back to the hall, picking up the hat from the hat stand and heads back to the lounge. She sits back down on her comfy chair again, then examines the hat.

'Right, there is a Gardenia, a white rose, and a green flower. Not sure what that is,' she murmured to herself.

Clara flips through the pages, looking for the G letter word hoping to find the Gardenia page and its meanings.

'Aha! Here is it, G. Gardenia means... Good luck, wow! That is very good news to hear, we all want that. Now next one is a white rose meaning,' she flips through the pages looking for a R for rose, 'A red one means love, I knew that... right a white rose means loyalty, innocence, and purity. Not bad. So, I should be alright for going shopping with this hat today. Now back to G,' and finding it she says, 'A green flower, whatever is that going to be? Here it is... it does have green flower meanings. This one is another good sign by the looks of it, this means good fortune and youth. I could do with some good luck; I am not sure about the others. In time will tell, maybe it will happen in the future, I just know today is going to be a good day, I just feel it. After the roof stress problem, and the time with Delia, now time for me to have a treat. Hopefully with my pretty yellow hat, with flowers on. Whatever can go wrong? All I am doing is going down to the village to get a few groceries and then coming back, and getting on with the garden and housework, possibly treating myself to sticky bun or two, or a bar of chocolate.'

Clara lifted up her blouse to reveal her stomach, she looked at it, then seeing it looked plump, she pinched her stomach to feel how much fat she had there.

'Hmm a bit lumpy. I am not happy with that, maybe have a smaller cake and no chocolate. That will not be the same as a big sticky bun with lots of icing on it. Or… maybe today a knight in shining armour with pick me up and whisk me off to his castle on the hill and make love to me all night long… mmm fine chance of that happening at my age. I can only dream can't I?'

Clara putting down her blouse and tucking into her warm woollen shirt.

Clara giggled to herself. 'Come off it Clara, he would be far too young for you. Now! If… I was younger then things would be quite normal to be whisked off by this knight in shining armour, but I am not!'

Clara came back to reality, 'I must get going, it will soon be lunch time and I must get back

and put on my stew ready for tonight's dinner.'

Clara got up from her chair and came into the hall. She found her coat she was going out in hanging on the hall coat stand and slipped it on. Glancing at the mirror nearby, she noticed that she did not have her hat on, from seeing in the mirror her bare head was missing a hat, she went back to fetch her hat. She quickly put it on her head, picked up her awaiting handbag which she left there last night ready for today's shopping, and her woven carrier bag beside it, and marched outside through the door slamming the door, and strolling towards the village shops, to do her normal shopping.

Her first shop she was going to, was the baker, Monroe's Bakeries. to buy her usual bloomer loaf of bread – the bloomer loaf was her favourite kind.

She pushed open the door, as she entered the shop, she noticed a queue of customers in front of her, she stood behind the long queue, patiently waiting for her turn to come. This was her fascinating and enjoyable pastime watching what the other customers were buying: some had a massive amount of cakes and bread rolls, and others only one item purchase.

An old lady had one loaf only, probably a person like herself, she thought. A tall woman was the next person in the queue, she went bolding forward, with a very determined look on her face, she started demanding to Gina.

'I must have a large chocolate cake,' she shouted her order at Gina. 'I only want to give my Auntie Darcel a LARGE chocolate cake. My auntie Darcel, (the name was used after her mother's favourite film star in it) is coming to tea on Sunday and would walk out of my house shouting if she DID NOT get her large chocolate cake. My auntie, she is very adamant, she is used to being given her LARGE CHOCOLATE CAKE every time she comes over for tea.'

Gina did her best, unfortunately for the woman she was given the last chocolate cake in the shop, but as it was very small, Gina said she could have it for half price because of the size.

'Ok it will have to do, Auntie Darcel will never forgive me, and possibly she will never speak to me again.' growled the angry woman.

Gina put the small chocolate cake in a brown bag, she put on a brave face for this angry woman and was scared what she was going to do next. The angry woman snatched the bag, out of Gina's hand, slammed down some coins on the counter and stormed out.

The rest of the customers in the shop, were flabbergasted at this woman's behaviour as they watched her losing her temper with the poor shop assistant. Hopefully they were not going to upset this woman and she was not getting angry with them, as they all felt very shaken at the whole experience.

The atmosphere of the shop went very quiet for a while.

Gina looked very shaken at this horrible experience, in fact shaking with fright, but she was unable to stay in the shop. She left the counter and went to the back of the shop to calm down and found five minutes to compose herself again. All the customers in the shop, just stood waiting and hopefully for Gina to return, not knowing what to do about this horrible experience in the shop.

Gina eventually came back looking red eyed, upset and sad, but she carried on in a business-
like manner.

'Yes, next customer please.' she smiled putting on a brave face, but worried and hope that this was not repeated with the next customer, by with a bit strain tried to be being cheerful but glad the angry woman had not returned for another rant.

Suddenly out of the blue, burst in was a four-year-old goes into the shop, and walked straight across, over to the counter.

There was no parent were in sight of being there, but she ignoring the queue waiting there in front of her – she was too young to know about the queueing system.

'Mummy want ten cakes, all wrapped up please.' she said

politely.

Gina was astounded about this child who appeared from nowhere. She was glad the child broke the ice of the nasty atmosphere that this woman had left Gina feeling in the shop and lighten the somewhat bad feeling that feeling that was left in the shop.

Gina asked, 'Do you mean our butterfly cakes, or something else?'

'Butterfly or moth cakes, that will do.' said the young child, innocently, in a grown-up reply.

This cheered up Gina with the moth word of the cakes. She had never heard that before. She did what the young child wanted and wrapped them up, in a brown paper bag, and handed the bag across to the young girl, who stood on her tiptoes to reach for the bag, normally Gina would have put the cakes in a box, to stop them getting squashed and damaged. But because of the earlier incident, she was flustered and just popped them in a bag instead. The child gave Gina a pound note from her small purse that she got by managing to reach down to her large carrier bag, and putting down on the counter, she quickly ran out of the shop.

This cheered up the four remaining people left in the shop. They now all appeared much more relaxed, after the grumpy mother had left, and the strange child coming in was a tonic to them all standing there.

At last Gina smiled, back at the next customer: a young man who wanted to buy a delicious birthday cake for his mother with the words HAPPY BIRTHDAY MUM written in beautifully pink icing sugar on a white iced cake, decorated with different coloured flowers dotted all over it.

Gina by now was feeling confident and relaxed, and

wrapped up this cake in a pink cardboard box, tied neatly in a pink ribbon, ending with a bow on the top of the box. He paid for it and walked proudly out of the shop with his purchase.

Clara smiled at the young man as he walked past her. He smiled back, which pleased Clara, that he noticed her and made her feel maybe being old she could do it, but a younger woman would give the impression she wanted more from a young man to be noticed again, first by Albert and then this young man, Clara realising how much she missed her own family, but soon forgot when the queue became closer to her turn. She was wondering whether to order a cake for herself now her birthday was looming closer, but she wanted to forget her age and concentrate on getting her bread. But the lady in front of her was dithering about what she wanted, was it ten doughnuts or ten iced buns. Eventually after Gina suggested what about chocolate eclairs, the lady then decided on ten chocolate eclairs.

'Is that all madam?' asks Gina brushing her hair out of her face with the back of her arm, but keeping her hands from touching the sticky eclairs, glad to resolve her dilemma situation.

Clara had finally arrived at the counter with her turn.

Gina was now tired and fed-up with those difficult customers and the angry woman earlier with the chocolate cake, she was looking as if she just wanted to go home and put her feet up. Gina was always there loyal but these days she was looking old for age, whatever that was. She going to retire or was she just old from the stress of awkward customers, Clara wasn't sure.

'Can I have that bloomer loaf?' she asked Gina pointing to her usual bloomer loaf.

'Do you mean this loaf?' asked Gina, picking up a loaf that

she knew was older than the rest and needed to be sold that day.

'No! the one behind that one, please' insisted Clara.

Gina reluctantly picked up the fresh on from that morning bake, she knew from the look of the pattern she remembered had a beautiful stripe down the middle of it, that it was the fresher one that day.

'Perfect,' remarked Clara, pleased to have the loaf she required, not the one Gina wanted her to have.

She knew that shop assistants would try and give the customers an old item, making sure that the stale or older items go first, but Clara was having none of this dry loaf. A dry one would be perfect for breadcrumbs but not for her toast at breakfast time.

'Lovely, every morning I have it toasted with butter and marmalade for breakfast.' She murmured to Gina.

'Yes! agreed Gina, now was so bored with her work today, that she was secretly yawning behind Clara's back.

'Now what else do I need from here?' Clara said looking down at her notepad of her shopping list.

'No! nothing more from here. How much will that come to, Gina?' enquired Clara, staring hard at Gina wondering at the same time, did she have a husband or boyfriend? Gina was getting on, to Clara thought she looked about fifty-five, she should be married by now.

'That will be two shilling and sixpence,' said Gina, yawning again, this time in front of Clara.

'Are you tired?' Clara asked Gina.

'Yes.' snapped Gina grumpily, handing Clara her change.

Somewhat surprised at Gina reply, she quickly thanked Gina, adding: 'See you again on Wednesday,' knowing she will be back again for another loaf again.

Clara left the shop and wandered down the road, passing the newsagent shop. As she passed the window of the newsagent shop, she noticed a bright yellow notice. She stopped and stared at it.

Clara put on her reading glasses and then read it out loud.

'AN AUCTION AT THE TOWN HALL ON THE 15TH OF JULY AT TWO O CLOCK SHARP. BUYER AND SELLERS WELLCOME. Tea and coffee afterwards.'

Oh, an auction, I have never been to an auction before. I don't know what it is all about, she

thought. Clara carried on thinking about the auction, and thought I really need a picture or two. She soon forgot about it, and went on her way to the green grocers, when she got there, she saw outside displayed, several extra items she wanted to buy. Aha, raspberries, cherries and

strawberries. How much? Maybe that will be my treat for the weekend. She strolled through the door this time as the door was open.

Looking around she noticed more boxes of raspberries and strawberries inside the shop. I mustn't forget my potatoes, carrots, cabbages, turnips, and onions. I do love strawberries, that reminds me: more cream from the milkman in the morning.

'Hello, Mrs Fortesque,' smiled Albert, who was busy with another customer but had time to be cheerful and friendly to other customers coming into his shop.

Albert was the only son of the owner, Cuthbert, who was getting on in years. Cuthbert still did his normal share of the work during the day, but had to go home to look after his wife Betty, who could not get out and about as much as she used to. Cuthbert's other children were married and had moved away, so it was up to Albert to carry on the family business, which he did not mind. Albert, who was married to Betty, had two other children, both at Secondary Modern school, doing their O levels: Petal and Mary. Petal was the youngest, kind and sweet, just happy to play and enjoy being a girl with her friends, not interested in knowing what she wanted to do when she left school. Mary was the eldest bossy, all she wanted to be a Matron or something in that line.

Clara moved closer to the raspberries, examining them just to make sure they were fresh and pink, otherwise if they were white with no flavour, she would not contemplate them. They did look sweet and ripe; she would have them. I wonder how many boxes I need... I also wonder how many strawberries boxes should I buy too.

Albert was now free to see to Clara with her green grocers list and he came over to enquire her green grocers needs.

'Now Mrs Fortesque what do you want today? Weather's not nice yesterday, but it does look nicer today, don't you think?' asked Albert.

'Yes,' agreed Clara, smiling and staring at this kind man she had known for years, since he was a young boy, playing in his father's shop, with his mother at the back sorting out the fruit and vegetables, making sure they were suitable for shop customers.

'Can I have my usual, but can I have two boxes of raspberries and one box of strawberries as well as my usual vegetables?' asked Clara, looking for her purse in her handbag.

'Of course, I have some lovely red onions, as well as the brown ones. Would you like to try these this time?' asked Albert, busy weighing the vegetables that Clara had asked for.

'Thank you, yes, they do look lovely.' agreed Clara.

Albert packed all the items that Clara wanted.

'Can I pop them in your basket?' asked Albert, trying to be helpful.

'Yes, thank you.' said Clara, smiling at Albert who had bent down to put the fruit and vegetables into her bag.

Clara noticed when Albert bent down, he was losing his hair, and getting a bald patch on the top of his head. She also noticed when he handed her the bags his fingers were all yellow. Clara knew that meant he was a smoker, as her husband Michael was a smoker once. He did have yellow fingers, so she associated this with smoking, from the nicotine from the cigarettes, but they soon disappeared when he left off his cigarettes five years later and gave it up after they got married, much to Clara's relief. Clara has a neighbour who has a bad cough from something, was it because he smoked – he also had yellow fingers too. It made Clara think, should she tell Albert about Michael who once smoked, and her neighbour who had a bad cough, maybe from smoking?

She said nothing and when her purchases had been packed and paid for, she walked away from the green grocers worried about Albert's health.

Clara walked on, towards the butchers, but then decided not to get any meat that day. In fact, she thought I really do not like meat. Maybe I should eat more eggs and skip meat and drink more tea and biscuits instead.

Eventually Clara arrived back home, and went into the kitchen, and put away the fruit and vegetables in the larder. She put on the kettle and sat down thinking about Albert, and his yellow fingers.

The next day was the day of the auction, and Clara marched down the road heading towards the town hall. Outside it was bustling with people carrying pictures and men moving large furniture in and out of the Town Hall.

She noticed that the main entrance was the way into the Auction rooms with a big black notice saying TO THE AUCTION ROOMS, stuck on the main door with a black arrow written underneath this notice.

She walked through the door. It was very noisy with all the hustle and bustle of the place. Clara went over to a large lady sitting on a chair who was talking to a smartly dressed gentleman standing up beside her talking and pointing to the pictures on the wall.

'Excuse me to interrupt. I came here for the auction. Where do I go?' she asked the lady sitting down.

The man who was talking to the lady in the chair butted in in a loud authoritative manner said 'Over their madam. Go through that door there – there are plenty of chairs in there. You can sit down or stand up, whatever you want, just wait for the auctioneer to start.'

'Right thank you, said Clara.

He then carried on talking to the lady, and lost interest in Clara who now felt a little uncomfortable about his abrupt manner.

Clara soon found the door. She walked through there were hundreds of people mingling about.

Clara sat down feeling nervous and excited the same time about the whole experience. She just looked at everything going on, at least she admitted, I am out of the house, not spending any money. In fact, maybe a cheap day out. I am very lucky indeed; in here it is warm and friendly and with lots of company. I should do this more often, she thought.

The noise gradually stopped, and the auctioneer started

bidding.

The items were fascinating and different, Clara was loving every minute of it. She noticed next to her a very large man with an enormous fat stomach, stretched out on an armchair. The armchair looked very comfortable and homely. She was now wishing she had this chair in her lounge room, so she could slouch on it and talk to people on her telephone.

That poor man, he looks so uncomfortable that he must be having to have this large stomach of his. He must be so unhappy with his trousers being so tight.

The man with the fat stomach, hand kept going up and down, nearly knocking poor Clara out of her seat, nearly hitting her yellow hat with flowers on it. His hand went up and down with his card of numbers written on it, bidding for lots of items.

Where did he get his card from? thought Clara.

She noticed on the table nearby a pile of white cards with big, black, bold numbers printed on them. Maybe I better have one, she thought, wondering if this is the way people went about buying something. I do not want anything at all they all look like rubbish to me, she thought, adding: I haven't seen all the items, in the auction, but I do need a picture for the lounge, and one for the bedroom. Michael will love me to buy a picture that I like, he knew he was selfish sometimes and wanted his own taste in pictures, not mine, so I will treat myself with a picture of something with lots of colours in, or a still life. Maybe... if there is a painting of a naked man, I may consider it. Clara had a giggle to herself, if I did what would my children think when they come into my bedroom after my days to clear up. My grandchildren, I expect. Say,

'I never thought Granny loved sex, in fact, I would never thought Granny and Grandad did that!' Maybe not a good idea

– I will stick to something more conservative!

By now Clara hat was beginning to feel hot and itchy. She had in her hand the bidding card, so, she scratched her head at the same time still holding her card near her head, accidently waving the card about it the air.

The auctioneer shouted out loud, who was glad to sell this enormous ugly vase.

'The lady at the back wearing the yellow hat, thank you madam for bidding for this beautiful vase. 'The auctioneer said lying about the vase.

'Going, going, gone, to the lady with yellow hat with flowers on!' he shouted banging firmly down his gavel on the big oak table in front of him, thankful someone had bought this big ugly vase, when the previous day no one wanted it!

Clara whispered to the man next to her, a young man in his twenties on the other side of Clara's chair.

'What a horrible vase,' she admitted to him, 'Who on earth would buy that ghastly vase,' she whispered to him.

The young man agreed with her.

Did he say a lady with a yellow hat with flowers on? Clara thought to herself. I have a yellow hat with flowers on? It wasn't me, I haven't bided for it, she thought feeling relieved it wasn't her.

'That poor woman who bought that revolting vase, and it is enormous, stupid woman.' said Clara angrily.

A tall man came over to Clara later on, the same man she spoke to earlier about where to go to see the auction came over to see Clara.

'How are you going to pay for your vase, madam?' asked the tall man.

'What vase?' asked Clara puzzled.

'The vase you just put your hand up for.' said the man.

'I wasn't that woman with a yellow hat, I do not want any vase!' shouted Clara, feeling annoyed about the vase that the man accused her in buying.

Someone else had bought it, not her. Go away horrible man, she said to herself, and leave me alone. By now Clara had removed her hat and had it on her lap. She is staring down at it she was now panicking about the vase – was he right or did he have the wrong woman?

'Madam you have a yellow hat, and you have bought the vase, I am afraid you must pay for it. This is an auction, you bided for it, and you must take it away. Sorry madam that is the rules.' demanded the man, now fed up with this stupid, difficult, old woman.

My oh my, what have I done, I bought a vase. I was just saying to the young man who was sitting next to me how horrible it was.

The tall auctioneer man stood looking down angrily and annoyed as he was waiting for Clara to pay for it.

'I have no cash on me, just a cheque book, I just hope I have enough money' Clara admitted.

'That will do, but madam, next time bring with you someone with sense and understanding and knowledge about auctions. If you bid something, then that is yours to keep. No returning like a purchase in a shop. What will your husband think about this when you get home? I presume your husband is still there to knock some common sense into your head?' he said grumpily.

'I have no husband; I am a widow.' admitted Clara sadly.

'I am so sorry. I did not mean to upset you. Have you any family nearby who could help you, the next time you come?' he said apologetically, 'Mrs...'

'Mrs Clara Lucinda Fortesque, my husband, the late Mr Michael Fortesque, was a very known businessman in this town.' says Clara talking with a lump in her throat feeling sad at not having her husband to stick up for her and feeling very sad and alone.

Clara got out her cheque book from her handbag and wrote on her lap.

'How much is it going to be?' she asked the man.

'That will be three hundred pounds' said the man.

Clara realised that she may not have enough but she wrote it anyway. He won't know until Friday – three days to clear the cheque.

Clara handed over the cheque to the man, who quickly put in his back trouser pocket, and left Clara now with this vase, sitting opposite on the table nearby, to be taken from the auction room, now it has been paid for. The young man who was sitting next to Clara earlier came over to her.

'Can I help you bring it home?' he asked Clara.

'Really?' said a surprised Clara 'I would be most grateful, as I possibly cannot take this home.' admitted Clara.

The young man told her he would pick up the vase later, at four o'clock sharp. He left Clara alone. Clara now shed a tear of relief for this young man's help, and sadness at buying this horrible, expensive vase.

Clara stayed sat on a chair, until four o'clock when the young man would come back. She watched her watch ticking slowly by, looking up at the people now and again. She really did not mind waiting, it gave her a chance to relax in the knowledge she was looked after by this helpful young man. She enjoyed watching the people walking away with their chosen items, some very small, possibly rings in those small boxes, and other people with bigger items. This man carrying a stuffed ape, accompanied by his lady friend, also carrying a small one that looked like a stuffed squirrel, not at all Clara choice. The vase was an easier option, being an item to blend in with her other vintage objects.

Just as Clara had got used to being there and forgotten about worrying about the time, and she was just happy sitting in a warm place, knowing eventually she was going home, with a kind young man was coming back, he suddenly appeared.

'Hello! I am here for your help.' he said smiling.

Clara looked down at her watch, he had done exactly what he said four o'clock sharp.

'Oh, hello,' said Clara pleased to see a friendly person after meeting two grumpy men today.

'Right,' he said, picking up the large vase.

The vase looked very light the way he was holding it. He stood clutching the vase.

Do follow me. We can put the vase into the boot of my car and I will take you and the vase back to your home. I will take it into your house, and then you or your husband can put it in a suitable place.' he said grinning.

The vase was now getting difficult to hold, and too heavy for him, as he was still standing holding of it.

'Thank you again.' said Clara gratefully.

The young man carried the vase with Clara following behind him, happy she had help, but angry with her yellow hat for causing all this trouble and making her have an itchy head, which was the cause of the hat incident.

Luckily for the young man, all the doors were still wide open for him to carry it out. He only had to walk a few yards from the auction rooms to his car. They arrived at his car which was his Mini car.

He stopped near the boot, and asked Clara. 'Do you mind getting the keys from my coat pocket. The one on my left side please.' he said still holding the vase steady.

Clara willingly put her hand in his jacket pocket, feeling around for his car keys. She did that and noticed while getting the keys his pocket contained some coins, but she left those there and took out the keys.

Adding: 'Could you open the boot too please.'

Clara fiddled about the boot keyhole, prising it open, lifted the boot up, revealing inside a spare tyre, a first aid kit and a rollup mac, umbrella, and a spare rug for the ground to sit on.

'Thanks.' he said.

He carefully put the vase down into the boot putting it on its side with the rug wrapped safely around it and slammed down the boot.

'Where do you live Mrs... I presume you are married. I did notice your ring, in fact your beautiful rings.' he admitted.

'Mrs Clara Fortesque, yes, I am married, yes, the rings were given to me by my late husband.' admitted said Clara.

'I am so sorry to hear that about your husband. When we get in, please tell me where you would me to put the vase,' asked the young man 'Jump into the car Mrs Fortesque and I will take you home, hold on I will open the door for you.'

He went around to the passenger side and opened the car door for Clara. Clara got in and sat down next to the young man in the passenger seat, feeling very cosy and secure, now having a kind man's present for a short time. It was something Clara had missed since her Michael had passed away, and her children had moved far away. Clara enjoyed the car journey her only luxury was a taxi, she did use buses and trains, but she was alone on theses. She missed Michael taking her out to her favourite haunts.

'Now Mrs Fortesque where do you live?' he asked.

'Of course, sorry, I live at thirty-four Springfield Close, Merivale.' She said.

'I know that area it is not far from the golf course in Hanningfield.' admitted the young man.

'That is right, my husband was very lucky to have a golf course so close, and nearby is a beautiful country walks where I took the children for a brisk walk to keep them amused, while Michael was playing there.'

The drive towards Clara's house was very interesting. She could enjoy this journey, going the normal way to her home and not via a bus or train, when she had to struggle home with a laden of heavy shopping, as sometimes her fruit and vegetables were somewhat difficult to manage on her own. If only she had this young man was always in her life, then living would be something to look forward to, and when anything goes wrong in her house, she has this young man to ask for his thoughts and experiences, and hopefully always close by if any emergency happens. She had no choice but to enjoy this short time with him!

Eventually they arrived back to Clara's house. The long drive towards Clara house was strange, coming down the drive in a car, which was driven by a stranger and not a family member was different. The car drew up, near the entrance of Clara's house.

The young man waited for Clara to get out first, but noticed she was slow, so he jumped out and went around the passenger side and helped Clara get out. She stood up and brushed down her dress that had managed to ride up her legs showing her bare stocking legs, which the young man did not notice. He went to the boot of the car and opened it.

Clara said to him. 'I will just open the front door for you.'

He waited till Clara's front door was wide open, and carefully took out the large vase out of the boot, picking it up and walked towards the door, with Clara holding the door wide for him to take the vase through.

He came into the hallway, still holding the vase, asking 'Where you want the vase, Mrs Fortesque?'

'Oh, dear! I have no idea, let me think,' she murmured 'Over there is a large table in the corner, could you put it on there, the table it wide enough for it.'

'Right you are,' he said.

He carried it slowly across to the table carefully putting it down, and then standing back and looking at it.

'The more I look at it the vase the nicer it is.' he admitted.

Mrs Forteque stood beside him and said, 'Do you know young man, I quite like it too. That vase looks alright on that table. In fact, it could do with a couple of Pampas Grasses in it and I think it will fit in nicely with the rest of the décor.' admitted Clara, glad she liked the vase a tiny bit more now she was away from grumpy auction people and having this young man here was nice and comforting,

'Yes, maybe not such a bad buy after all.' admitted this young man, being complimentary.

'Now that is done and dusted, will you take something for your troubles?' asked Clara.

'No, please, it was a pleasure and a privilege.' he admitted 'I only came to the auction to get away from my stressful job.'

'What do you do then?' asked Clara.

'I work for an electronic company who wants me rushing here and rushing there for them. I work with their van, taking electronic item to people's business. Some of the items are heavy electronic appliances. I get very exhausted; the boss is very grumpy and has his own problems at home and takes it out on me.' he admitted.

'Well, young man, I do need someone to take me out sometimes, but I can only offer you a small amount of money, and I hope you do not mind me asking what your accommodation is like.' informs Clara.

'I live in one room in a small house. They also feed me, as they only can offer me a room, with meals which suit me, and then the owners are a young couple who are very easy going and do not mind me staying there. It suits them just staying there three days and spend four days with my parents and help them with shopping and their business.' Oliver admitted.

'Would you like to live here for three days a week and help me? Also be a butler and take me sometimes in your Mini, I just love your car, it so beautiful and cosy.' admitted Clara.

'I would love that, could I help you with your beautiful garden?' asked Oliver excited at leaving his job.

He did not mind having a smaller amount of money when he was happy, this was a good idea, being happy was better than being rich and unhappy.

'Oh yes, lovely!' said a pleased Clara, getting excited with having this young man back in her life, and seeing him, who is willing to help her with the garden now, she was glad to take a back seat on her garden.

Oliver could give her some fresh idea regarding the garden, and if he liked to grow some vegetables and plant some more fruit trees, raspberry and gooseberry bushes giving her fruit for making more pies for her friends and neighbours, this is perfect to a very bad and stressful day at the auctions.

'I am an excellent cook.' He admitted.

'Oh yes! Perfect!' admitted Clara clapping her hands with glee.

'Now let's get down to your name, I did not catch it?' enquired Clara.

'Oliver Morley Lawrence Pearl.' he said.

'Ooh! Perfect just a lovely name.' admitted Clara, pleased that the bad day of the vase buying had brought this nice young man into her life.

'Tell me all about yourself, Oliver, I would love to know more about you, as you are living in my house soon,' admitted Clara, looking at Oliver with warmth in her eyes, adding 'I need to know a little about yourself first.'

'I was born here in this village, by a lovely midwife called Winnie. I went to a public school, in Winchester, until I was eighteen years old, and then left school with seven o levels and two A levels. After that I went to Chester University, studying English and Business studies. I wanted to work in helping people start their own business but decided if I needed to help my parents in their business, I would take a part time job. My family wanted me to work full time in their business, but I said I would have a compromise and have four days with them and my own time in another job. But now it is so stressful, but it is good money. I would love to help you Mrs Fortesque.' said Oliver.

'Call me Clara now, and we can come to some arrangement about the money, accommodation, food, and uniform, but there is one but: can you provide your own car? I have no driving licence, or car, and it would be nice for you not to have my car, as it would have to stay here, and as you are helping your parent, you need to have your own car.' admitted Clara.

'Certainly.' agreed Oliver.

'Now young man, have you time for a cup of tea? I can show you your accommodation, and we can make a list, what you are able to do, and what I would like you to do. I am looking forward to having you around for your company and help. Of course, I will need more idea about your family, and could you provide me with a character reference? Now, the telephone is over there,' said Clara pointing to the telephone on the side table 'You are very welcome to use it anytime. I will just go and put the kettle on, unless you would like coffee?' asked Clara.

'No, a cup of tea will be perfect.' he admitted.

'Good, and a piece of my favourite gingerbread, unless you want a biscuit?' asks Clara, smiling.

'Great! My Gran made that when she was here, and Grandad loved his Battenberg. By the way, Clara, can I ring the Boss when I have checked the car?' asked Oliver.

'Yes, of course go ahead. My husband's favourite was Battenburg too; we are going to get along just fine, aren't we Oliver?' admitted Clara, getting up to go to the kitchen.

Clara disappeared into the kitchen to make her tea, while Oliver went to his car, to check the car and lock it. In he came and went across and phoned his boss and told him he was going to give a week notice, as it was a Friday, he would finish that Friday the thirteenth of this month.

Whee... went the kettle. Oliver came into the kitchen, while Clara was busy getting the tea ready.

'Please make yourself comfortable and I will bring in the tea.' said Oliver butting in 'Leave it on a tray and I will bring it for you, Clara.' he said kindly.

Clara did what she was told to do and went into the lounge and sat down waiting for Oliver with the tray of tea things for them both to enjoy. Oliver brought the tray in five minutes later and started to serve tea: his first mission of being a butler. Oliver knew that his family would be very proud of him. He hoped that this was the start of a different career, taking him to new horizons and new exciting prospects of life, after Clara. He knew this was paramount for Clara, and he could go to other places of work in the future. He may consider being a chauffeur of a butler, he wasn't sure, for now.

Clara sat back in her comfy chair, and now felt that at last life was going to be a lot easier and happier for her.